An Unsinkable Love

By Terri Benson

An Unsinkable Love

Copyright © 2012, Terri Benson

Edited by Nerine Dorman

Cover Art by Casey Winterbower/Nimbll.com

PUBLISHER'S NOTE:

Terri Benson

Dedication

This book is dedicated to Rick, my junior-high-school sweetheart and husband of more than thirty five years. You've listened to my plots, helped me with research, put up with late dinners--or none at all, a dirty house and reams of paper scattered from room to room without complaint. You gave me encouragement and cocktails, and always said you knew I could do it. But just because I did, don't think it's over yet. I've already scheduled more writing, more cocktails, and more of you for another thirty years.

Acknowledgements

Thanks to:

The Colorado West Writer's Workshop, especially Evil Editor Jan the Grammarian, for your insight, critique and cheerleading.

Nerine Dorman for her efforts to make this book the best it can be, and for allowing me to share it with the world.

And most of all, many thanks to Linda Weber, my BFF and Reading Buddy, who selflessly reads and reads and re-reads my manuscripts, offering advice, comfort and chocolate. Without you, this story never would have made it to the light of day. WooHoo!

Foreword

On April 15, 1912, at 11:40 PM the luxury liner *Titanic* struck an iceberg and sank in the north Atlantic. One thousand five hundred seventeen souls were lost. No one can ever know the effects this tragedy will have on history--what accomplishments, good and bad-- might have been. Those stories lie forever buried in the cold, dark depths.

Chapter 1

Thursday, April 11, 1912. Queensland, Ireland

Bree stared across choppy water at the mammoth ship. Did she dare? She glanced over her shoulder, searching for signs of pursuit. It was only a matter of time before they realized she was gone. If she didn't make up her mind quickly she wouldn't have any say in the matter. She took a deep breath and stepped up to the ticket window.

"I'd like a third class ticket." *Please, please let it not be too much.*

A pimply-faced clerk looked down his long nose at her. "That'll be seven pounds, miss, and you had better hurry. They're loadin' the last tender right now."

Seven pounds! It would leave her with next to nothing. How would she survive in America? "Excuse me. I'll be right back."

"Like I said, you better hurry--White Star don't wait on the likes of us."

Bree stepped away from the window and brushed away tears threatening to overflow. What should she do now? She couldn't go back, wouldn't go back, not ever. But to start out with no money? Bree knew the foolishness of that, but did she have a choice?

She slumped against the wall next to a hedge of large yew trees, her small battered trunk leaning drunkenly against her thigh. There had to be a way. She closed her eyes, laid the tips of her fingers on the warm, gold cross at her neck and prayed, "Please, God. I beg of you, don't make me go back."

A sudden gust rustled the yews and between the branches she saw two men on the other side, arguing. The wind shifted toward her.

"Damnation, Jack. Why'd you let them off the boat?" The speaker, a burly, sunburned, middle-aged man, bent toward the other with a stern expression. He wore a black wool uniform with three rows of gold braid circling the cuffs, and a double row of brass buttons down the front of his hip-length jacket. A visor cap was cupped under his elbow, a word embroidered across the brim in gold thread.

The shorter man, dressed more casually in work pants and a dark Shetland sweater, snapped, "Well, if I'd known they had no intention of coming back, Reggie, I wouldn't have. But Thomas said he'd been told to help Martha carry some fabric, and I didn't see any reason to doubt them."

"Damn it, that leaves us in a tight spot. We can't make six days at sea without at least one competent tailor. Old Thorpe can't do the work anymore. I knew I should have replaced him before we left. These shakedown voyages are always trouble. And the hoity-toities we have on board are bound to make every sort of demand for alterations or last-minute fixes. I'd best start checking with the shops here. Perhaps someone with at least basic skills will be available on short notice. You get back to the tender and see to it no one else jumps ship, or you'll be doing their work and your own besides."

"Yes, sir, Mr. Purser, sir," Jack said with a grin, clearly not intimidated by the older man.

Reggie half turned and peered past Bree's hiding place, already searching the cobbled street. With another pat on her cross and the murmured hope she wasn't making a mistake taking the overheard conversation for an answered prayer, she did something she'd never have considered before today. Bree stepped into the man's path, chin raised, stretching her five feet two inch frame as tall as possible. He nearly ran her down before stumbling to a halt. Bree stuck out her hand. "Sir, I understand you're looking for a skilled tailor."

Confusion washed over his face then he frowned as it must have dawned on him she couldn't have been aware of his snap decision. "Might be. How did you know?"

Bree dropped her hand. "I'm sorry. I didn't intend to eavesdrop, but I was standing behind the shrubs resting for a moment and happened to hear you mention it."

"Well, and what difference is it to you, young lady?" he asked, eyes narrowed.

"I'd like the job, sir." She struggled to keep the quiver of desperation from her voice.

The man's lips squashed down at the corners and his head tilted. It was an expression she'd seen before. With wild auburn hair cascading in curls down her back and fair skin sprinkled with freckles, she knew she appeared all of about twelve years old.

He pursed his lips and shook his head. "I'm sorry. I need someone experienced. We're far too busy to allow anyone to learn on the job. And our clients are very demanding."

"But you see, I *am* very experienced." Bree quickly turned to her trunk, snapped the latches and pulled out several garments, laying them across the open lid before he could object. "This is my work. I've been seamstress for the Lady Rothberry here for nigh on four years. If you doubt my word, the millinery is up the way a piece and Mrs. O'Malley will most certainly vouch for me. And I'm nearly nineteen, even though I don't look it."

The man regarded her with disbelief, then shook his head and picked up a soft, forest-green woolen cape. He rubbed his fingers over the beaded border, turning a seam out. Bending close, he scrutinized the tiny, neat stitches. He laid the cape down and picked up a crisp white shirtwaist. The buttonholes were exactly matched, heavy lace graced throat and cuffs, and the topstitching ran perfectly straight. Bree knew he wouldn't find any flaws in her work. She'd spent too many nights under her mother's tutelage to make mistakes, and Lady Rothberry hadn't tolerated anything less than perfection.

"The lace is mine as well, but I'm much to slow to make it for anyone but myself."

He peered down at her, taking in the lightweight wool suit she wore, his expression thoughtful. Bree was glad she'd worn her best outfit. It was quite fashionable, pieced from remnants of Lady

Rothberry's latest traveling suit. She'd planned to wear something old to avoid soiling her good clothes, but had changed her mind at the last minute.

"What is your name, young lady?"

"Bridget Barry, sir. But everyone calls me Bree."

"I'm not a man to make hasty decisions normally, but today I don't have the luxury of mulling it over. I'll give you a chance, Miss Barry. Do not disappoint me."

Bree nodded solemnly, but inside her stomach flip-flopped with excitement.

"I'm Reginald Barton, purser for the White Star Line. I'll take you on as seamstress. You'll be provided with a berth, uniforms, your meals and very little else."

She eyed him sharply and he smiled at his attempt at a jest.

"For the outrageous wage of three pounds, you'll work long hours providing our clients with exemplary service. The cruise lasts six more days. You'll be expected to stay in New York as our employee and make the return trip." He looked at his watch. "We sail in an hour." He pointed at her trunk as she finished repacking and flicked the latches. "It appears you're packed and ready to go?"

Bree couldn't believe her luck. Not only would she sail away from this place, she wouldn't have to spend any of her hard-earned funds to do it. She nodded. "Yes, sir. I have everything I need right here." Not just everything she needed, but everything she owned. She wouldn't tell him that, though. Her thoughts whirled. This was it--a once-in-a-lifetime chance to get away from the near-slavery she'd experienced most of her life. *America here I come, praise be to God!*

After he glanced at his watch again, Mr. Barton muttered to himself and flagged down an open carriage for hire. He hoisted her trunk into the boot and handed her in. As soon as he settled across from her, he urged the driver to make all speed down the quay toward the White Star dock. As the horse clip-clopped at a good pace over the jarring cobblestones, Mr. Barton inquired, "Are you from Queensland? You don't have much of a brogue."

"Yes, sir, I am. But my mother and I worked up at the manor, and Lady Rothberry didn't like Irish accents. She said it made us sound coarse and stupid. We needed the work." Bree shrugged. "There was a tutor at the manor until we learned to speak 'proper' English."

"What brought you to the wharf today?"

"Well, you see, I intended to purchase a ticket for the ship when I overheard you."

"I suppose I've done White Star out of a few pounds then." He smiled and Bree allowed her shoulders to relax. He wasn't going to change his mind.

They arrived barely in time to catch the paddle-wheeled tender *America* on its last run. Mr. Barton set her trunk down on deck and moved off to the tender's bridge to speak with the same man she'd seen him talking to on shore.

Alone on deck, Bree looked around nervously, unable to shake the fear her brothers or the Rothberrys would catch her at the last minute and drag her off. The tender gave a shrill whistle and pulled away from the dock at a snail's pace.

"Hurry, oh please, hurry," she whispered as she grasped the railing in a white-knuckled grip. No angry shouts rang out. No boots ran thudding down the dock. In a few moments she would be free. She would be on the most magnificent ship on the ocean, and it would be too late to stop her.

Once on board, she'd be beyond her family's reach. Now that mother was gone, she was absolved of any allegiance to the rest. Bree felt a sense of sadness, knowing her father and brothers wouldn't miss her nearly as much as her hard-earned wages they quickly spent at the pub. She inhaled the salty air and brightened a bit at the thought of never having to duck another backhand blow from her father, or clean up after her slovenly brothers, or beg the grocer to give her a piece of nearly turned meat at a discount so none would go hungry.

The demanding Lady Rothberry and her husband, who had recently started making unseemly demands of his own, would be easily forgotten. She'd never again have to beg Mrs. O'Malley to take back fabric her ladyship decided wasn't to her liking. She wouldn't be shut up in the drafty sewing room at the castle for days at a time either. The Rothberrys would search high and low for a new seamstress willing to put up with their calculated cruelty.

"How long will they all wonder what became of me?" she murmured. Her shoulders slumped as she realized they might not even care.

Bree stared up at the ship, its massive dark side filling her vision. Sunlight winked off hundreds of round windows dotting the ship's flank. Which would she be looking out? Her hand crept back to the

8

cross at her neck. *Dear God. The Titanic!* This grand ship would be
her home for the next several days. All the city of Queensland, and
probably all of Ireland, was chattering about how lucky they were to
be one of only two stops between Southampton and New York--and
now she, herself, would be part of the maiden voyage.

She craned her neck as she surveyed the highest decks. Four
immense smokestacks angled back, giving an impression the ship
moved at high speed, even though it sat at anchor. Two tall masts
bracketed each end of the long, dark hull--the upper superstructure
bright white. The bow appeared knife-sharp from a distance and the
delicately curved stern, which the newspapers called a "champagne
glass" shape, almost seemed out of place.

She jumped as a crate dropped heavily to the deck behind her.
Whirling around, she gaped in awe at the huge mountains of trunks
and bags piled on almost every square foot of the tender. The
deckhand sidled up, greedily eyeing her body. Bree drew back and
said, "Excuse me, what are all those bags for?" in an attempt to
distract him.

"Oi, thems mailbags, ducky. Hun'erds of 'em."

Bree stepped back as his pungent scent--unwashed body mingled
with old fish and cabbage--wafted toward her. He followed, gap-
toothed mouth leering, a dribble of black juice trailing down his
stubbled chin. She peered uneasily around his tightly stretched wool
jersey to see what had become of Mr. Barton, but he was nowhere in
sight.

"I'll let you get back to work. I wouldn't want you to get into trouble, since the purser is on board. I'm sure Mr. Barton would want to see everyone working hard." Bree inched away a few more steps.

The deckhand glanced cautiously over his shoulder and grunted. He sent a stream of tobacco juice squirting through the air toward the railing, wiped his chin on a grungy sleeve and sauntered off.

Bree sighed in relief and turned her gaze beyond the trail of foaming water. She surveyed Queensland from a different perspective than ever before. Her father was afraid of the sea, and refused to allow his family to set foot on a boat, let alone sail out into the *cobh*. Of course, he'd rarely let Bree or her mother outside the cottage except to go to work at the Rothberrys, unless he was along.

The town really was very pretty, stair-stepping up the hillside in terraces, golden stone kissed by the soft glow of sun through a faint foggy haze. The ancient buildings showed their age, but in a dignified way, like an old dowager who still carried herself well.

She tried to fix the sight in her mind, not knowing if she'd ever see it again, not willing to admit she might miss it someday. So much more of the world remained to been seen, starting with the fabled city of New York, then on to the whole grand continent of America. Bree couldn't help the smile that fair split her face. She turned and looped her arm around a support post, watching as they drew in under the shadow of the big liner. How tall it was! And how on earth would she get on it? Her question was answered only a few moments later when the tender tied up next to a nearly identical one and a gangplank ran out from one boat to the next. Several more gangplanks led from there into the liner, including covered ones angling steeply to upper decks. High above, ship's officers scrutinized paperwork and doctors briefly inspected the eyes of each passenger as they queued on small landings.

Closer by, another ramp led to a low, wide opening in the side of the *Titanic*, a scant dozen feet above water level. Mr. Barton appeared at her side and gathered her trunk, steering her across the gangplanks toward the lower opening.

There was a commotion before they stepped inside. Bree gasped as she observed three men awkwardly climbing a rope dangling off the ship. Below, sailors in a dinghy tried to shake them off. A group of drunken Irishmen hung over the railing and shouted encouragement in Gaelic. Without warning, the man highest on the rope slipped, hit the others and knocked them off as he fell. It happened so fast she didn't have time to scream.

Mr. Barton tapped her shoulder. "They'll be all right." Even as he spoke, sailors fished the soggy men out of the water and pulled them into the dinghy. The purser urged her on gently, giving her a steady arm as they crossed into the bowels of the ship.

It was noisy inside the corridor. Workers scurried every which direction like ants, trunks and bags slung over their shoulders. Dollies loaded with cartons and cases trundled across the polished wooden floor. Thuds, crashes, curses and shouts echoed the hallways. Corridors led off at regular intervals as they walked farther into the ship. Several times, they were forced to flatten against the cold metal wall and allow a dolly loaded with more supplies or trunks to pass. Small electric lights spaced along the ceiling gave off a feeble glow after the bright sunshine and it took a while for Bree's eyes to adjust.

Her guide turned left and right seemingly at random and they went up unmarked flights of stairs. A sudden flicker of fear nibbled at her confidence. What if she got lost and no one found her? It was silly, of course, but her life had taken such an incredible turn and she felt off balance. After she'd completely lost track of direction, Mr. Barton stopped in front of a narrow, blank wooden door, flanked by others equally nondescript.

The purser nodded at the doorway. "This is your cabin. You'll share it with a stewardess from second-class. The tailoring department is on F Deck. That's one deck below. Ask any steward you see and they can direct you. You'll need to report to your station as soon as we depart, so get your things put away." He set the trunk down and put out his hand. She shook it, embarrassed, knowing her palm was sweaty.

"Thank you, Mr. Barton."

He inclined his head slightly then headed down the hall before she could say more.

The shiny metal knob turned with a faint squeak. She stepped over a low sill and hoped she wouldn't trip over it every time she went through. Bree inspected her new lodgings. The room was even smaller than her bedroom at the castle, and didn't contain even one of the round windows. A set of bunk beds nearly filled the wall across from the door. A built-in wardrobe occupied the space on her right and to the left, a small sink and a table with two wooden chairs. A single light gave off the same wan glow as those in the corridors. The metal frame shielding the bulb cast a web of shadows. She stepped to the wardrobe, her heels echoing against the bare paneled walls, and opened the double doors. One side of the upper hanging section was packed with a jumble of dresses, the lower shelves stuffed with other pieces of clothing. Bree carefully placed her few belongings on the remaining wooden hangers and shelves.

As she slid her empty trunk under the lower bunk next to another battered case, the door squeaked open. She turned as a plump young woman in dark dress and white apron stepped in.

The newcomer was gazing down as she entered and pulled up with a start just before she ran into Bree. "Who're you?" Her bright blue eyes widened.

Bree bit her lip, uncomfortably shy, realizing she would be living with a total stranger. Having spent her entire life near the cottage or the castle, she'd rarely had the chance to meet a person she didn't know. "My name is Bridget Barry--my family calls me Bree. Mr. Barton hired me as a seamstress. I live in Queensland, or, well, I did. I might not ever go back." She realized she was babbling.

The girl flashed a wide smile. "I'm Annette Mallory. Anne. You just get on the ship?"

"Yes, a few moments ago, as a matter of fact. I hope it's all right I put my clothes in the wardrobe?"

"Sure. I'm in the lower bunk, so you'll have to take the upper. The bedding is folded on top. I'm glad to have a roomie. It can get kind of lonely even with all the people around. Come with me, I'll show you the facilities. We're lucky they're down around the corner.

Close enough to be convenient, but not right next door. I roomed next to them one trip, and I'll tell you, it was the worst. Noisy, and it didn't smell very good either. Of course, that was a different ship. Maxwell--he's a friend of mine from engineering--he says there'll likely be a lot of little problems to fix since this is the ship's first trip out. I hope it's nothing to do with the toilets." Anne paused for breath, removed her apron and hung it on one of a row of hooks next to the door.

Bree followed the young woman out into the hall and around a long bulkhead. There were people everywhere. Most were busy and focused on a task, but she saw a few couples or small groups talking and laughing, and assumed they'd finished their shifts for the day. The bathing facilities, one of three on their deck according to Anne, included several private water closets in a long line, with a pair of sinks in the corner. A large mirror occupying most of the wall space reflected tired green eyes, her face even paler than usual. A hallway alongside led to private bathing chambers, each with a large enameled tub.

"You'll have to see how your schedule works out. This place can be a mess at times when there are too many girls trying to get ready at the same time," Anne said, as they headed back to their cabin.

"I can imagine." Bree nodded, trying to envision bathing and dressing with so many strangers nearby.

As they returned to their tiny room, the floor vibrated and Bree heard a dull rumble. They were leaving--no turning back now. Mr. Barton's instructions came back to her. "Anne, can you tell me how to find F Deck?"

"Sure. Go right as you leave then two more rights. You'll see stairs ahead. Go down one level. I don't know where the tailor shop is exactly, but you can ask the deck stewards. They'll know."

Bree surveyed her suit, which was a tad rumpled. Her own design, it sported an ankle-length slim skirt topped by a long, belted tunic with deep V neckline. A high-necked white silk blouse with cravat and mock pearl buttons filled the gap. She'd have to wear the suit and her dainty lace-up kid boots until she received her uniform.

Bree followed Anne's directions and nodded shyly at other workers as they passed in the halls. She stepped off the last tread as a man dressed in casual flannels and twirling a straw boater on his finger barreled around the corner. Bree cringed, expecting to be knocked flat. With split-second reflexes, he threw his arm out, raised his shoulder and spun gracefully on his heel. He cleared the top of her head by a fraction of an inch before he fetched up against the bulkhead with a hard thump.

"Are you hurt?" Bree asked as she looked up. He towered a good foot taller, filling her vision with broad shoulders and a tantalizing V of bronzed skin framed by the open neck of his striped collarless shirt. She tipped her head back. Beyond his corded neck, she noted a firm chin. His well-formed lips stretched in a broad smile beneath a patrician nose and cobalt eyes gleaming with a combination of amusement and interest. A thatch of damp chestnut hair with pale highlights the color of ripe wheat complemented his deeply tanned skin. Realizing she was gawking quite rudely, Bree snapped her

15

mouth shut and felt the heat rise to her face.

He rubbed his shoulder. "I think I'll live." His cocky grin changed to chagrin after he noticed his straw hat. "Can't say the same for my boater, though." The brim hung loose from the crown, which had a jagged hole punched through it.

Bree knew her pale skin flushed deeper as his gaze traveled down to her toes and back up again, the cocky grin returning wider than ever. No one had ever studied her like that before. He was quite cheeky, but she couldn't help the shiver of excitement that flared through her body. It was far different from the fright that had plagued her when Lord Rothberry caught her in the gallery and made all those disgusting demands as his eyes fair stripped the clothes from her body.

Actually, it felt rather delightful to have a dapper young man admire her. With a start, Bree realized she'd allowed him to stare for far too long and tried to dampen her own excessive interest. She drew herself up to her full height, which put her nose one button below the fascinating bit of tanned skin. She affected her haughtiest Lady Rothberry tone and said, "Excuse me, sir," then whirled to continue on her way.

"Wait. I'm sorry. You took me by surprise. I hadn't expected to nearly run over a lovely young woman down here below decks. Please, let me introduce myself. My name is Malcolm DuMont. And you are?"

Bree halted and groaned quietly in frustration as she considered what she should do. She chewed her lip a moment, then turned to find him uncomfortably close and drew back a step. He really didn't seem the least bit contrite as he stood there, hand held out and eyebrow cocked.

Mr. DuMont obviously wasn't an employee. Bree wished she had been given instruction on how she should behave when speaking to a paying passenger. Mr. Barton would probably fire her on the spot if the man complained then she'd have no choice but to pay out her few coins for passage. He continued to watch her, head tipped to the side, as she hesitated.

With a resigned sigh she said, "Bridget Barry," and briefly shook his hand. "I don't mean to be rude, sir, but I do need to be about my business." Bree turned and scurried down the corridor, so flustered by the lingering warmth of his touch she could only hope she headed in the right direction.

* * * *

Malcolm watched the trim figure hurry down the hall. He smiled again, enjoying the view. Her long, wavy, auburn hair bounced with each step and the fabric of the slim skirt twitched over her hips in a most beguiling way. She dressed with style; the outfit could have come straight out of a Parisian design house, and *he* would certainly know. Of course, she was far too short for a couturier model, but he liked her small, shapely figure sheathed in the clinging outfit. He'd felt no stirring, no interest, in the tall, gangly women strutting through the French salons these past several weeks. His fingers itched to burrow into Miss Barry's long coppery hair, a welcome relief to the boyish bobs sported by the haute couture.

He reached back and scrubbed the short damp hair on the back of his neck. He would definitely need to find out more about Miss Bridget Barry. The *Titanic* might be huge, but there weren't all that many people in first class--and she definitely qualified as first class. He wondered vaguely what brought her below decks. As far as he knew, the only facilities here were squash and racquet courts, the pool and Turkish bath, and third class quarters.

Already devising his seduction, he whistled as he sauntered to the elevator to meet his mother for tea.

Chapter 2

Bree had to ask two different stewards before she found the tailor shop tucked away in the bow between the linen storage and soiled linen rooms. Mr. Thorpe, a thin, balding and taciturn man, introduced himself as the head tailor. He stood next to a long table, frowning and clearly unhappy to find his new subordinate a female.

"I suppose I'll have to make do with you, young lady. But mark my words, you will follow my instructions precisely. If I receive even one complaint about the quality of your work, you will be discharged, Mr. Barton or no Mr. Barton."

"Of course, sir. I won't disappoint you."

"I'm sure you will, but that's a burden I've borne before. All you young people are alike. More interested in meeting a wealthy passenger or carrying on with the other employees. Well, I won't tolerate such behavior. Are you clear on that?" He glared down at her through thick glasses perched on the end of his nose.

Bree nodded silently. With an abbreviated wave of his hand, he signaled her into a narrow wooden chair on the other side of his small desk. He opened a drawer in a cabinet behind him, retrieved a piece of White Star watermarked notepaper and scribbled a few lines.

Mr. Thorpe held the missive out to her and said, "Take this to the fitting room two doors down, on the other side of the soils room. Mrs. Unger will see to your uniform. Report back here as soon as she has you kitted out. Most of the day is wasted, but you can still manage a little work, I expect." He jerked his thumb over his shoulder.

Bree didn't think it fair to be blamed for not working all day, considering she'd only just arrived, but she held her tongue. A large heap of clothing sat on a worktable and she wondered if it represented only a half-day's work, or more.

He continued, "Tomorrow morning you will arrive by six o'clock sharp. I will assign your duties for the day. You will work until six o'clock in the evening, with one half hour for your midday meal. In addition, some of the passengers may require your services in the evening. You will remain in the employee recreation areas or dining rooms or your own room during the off hours so we can locate you when needed."

Bree was taken aback. She hadn't realized her every minute would belong to the company. Oh, well. It was only a few days. She wouldn't be any more under Mr. Thorpe's thumb than her father or Lady Rothberry.

* * * *

Mrs. Unger turned out to be the complete opposite of Mr. Thorpe. A jolly, plump and red-cheeked Irishwoman, she couldn't complete a sentence without fitting in a laugh somewhere.

"Come on in, dearie, and let me have a gander at you. Such a tiny thing you are. You say you're a seamstress? That's a foin thing, as I'm thinkin' you'll be needin' to take in wotever I can find for you here." She flitted around the room, muttering to herself as she pulled articles of clothing off shelves and shook them out, nodding or shaking her head depending on the suitability of the selection. A small pile accumulated on the table.

As she crossed the room to a row of cubbyholes, the heavyset woman called over her shoulder, "And wot size shoe are you wearin', dearie? I'd venture a size five, by the look of those foin boots you be sportin'."

Bree smiled in surprise. "Why, yes, that's right. How did you know?"

Mrs. Unger let out a brassy laugh and set chunky black shoes on the table next to the garments. She turned and put a thick arm around Bree's shoulders, and gave her a gentle hug.

"Ah, dearie, when you've been doin' this as long as I have, you get a feel for it. As I said, you'll be doin' some alterations on these uniforms. I haven't anything tiny enough for you, so I hope you don't mind stayin' up tonight to shorten the hems, and maybe takin' up the waist a wee bit."

Bree shook her head. "It won't be the first time I've whiled away the hours sewing into the night. At least this time it will be for me."

"You've got two dresses, and four aprons. Try to keep the dresses clean. You'll not be given any more and since we've no laundry on this ship, you'll have to wash them in the bath and dry them in your

21

room. There are two pairs of stockings, two caps, and the shoes. You'd best try everything on now so I can pin the dresses for you, and we can change the shoes if they don't fit."

Bree removed her suit, leaving on her combination undergarments, and slipped on the black dresses one by one. Mrs. Unger pinned up the hem and extra tucks on each side of the waist. While Bree removed her boots and picked up one of the heavy shoes, the woman ran her hand over the wool suit.

"This here's a foin piece of work. If it's yours, old Thorpe will be lucky to have you. His eyes are so bad, he don't dare do any of the fine work hisself."

The shoes had been worn previously, but showed only slight wear. With a shrug, Bree slid them on and pulled the laces tight. She took a few steps and found them clumsy and stiff, not at all like her soft, light boots. They would be serviceable, though and, once broken in, quite tolerable.

Mrs. Unger nodded her approval. "You're lucky *Titanic* is new. I've seen a few ships where the shoes and clothes were better suited for the rag picker than hard-workin' people." She bundled the clothing up and tied it with twine. "Will you be takin' these with you, or shall I send them to your cabin?"

"Mr. Thorpe asked me to return to work as soon as you were finished with me, so if you could send them to my cabin, I'll deal with the alterations this evening."

"That old slave driver. As if it would hurt to allow you a few hours to get settled," Mrs. Unger grumbled. "You go on then. I'll see to it. I expect I'll be seein' you by and by, dearie."

Bree went back to Mr. Thorpe and began work. As she finished one garment, Mr. Thorpe quickly filled her hands with another. The tedious chore didn't hold her attention. A button here, a few stitches there--her hands seemed to complete the tasks with no thought whatsoever. Her mind wandered to the near collision with the handsome and very upsetting man. His behavior had been quite impertinent. If they met again she would certainly put him in his place, passenger or no passenger. But while she devised several cutting comments, her body followed a different tack altogether. She squirmed in the hard chair and felt heat on her face as her unrepentant imagination conjured a vision of blue eyes lowering to hers, his smirking smile replaced by a tender, love-filled gaze.

She jerked and sucked in a deep breath as blood welled from a tiny pin hole. Her inattention had made her careless. She quickly stuck the finger in her mouth and sucked, not wanting to leave a bloodstain on the fine piece of lace. From under lowered lids, she stole a look at Mr. Thorpe to see if he'd noticed. As luck would have it, his back was turned. Mentally chastising herself for mooning over a stranger, she attacked the remaining sewing with a vengeance and put the annoying young man out of her mind. Almost.

Her back ached and her eyeballs felt dry as dust from the dim electric light when Mr. Thorpe grudgingly dismissed her for the day. Before she left, Bree begged needles, scissors, a measuring stick and matching thread to alter the uniforms.

He glared, his lips pressed together tightly then said, "I'll allow personal use of the equipment just this one time, but don't presume on my good nature again."

Bree bit her lip to keep from laughing at "his good nature."

The multitude of corridors and stairs were confusing and, after eventually making her way back up to E Deck where she stopped for a quick supper in a dining hall she happened upon, she took a wrong turn trying to find her cabin. While searching for a steward, she rounded a corner and found a large common area populated with several employees. The room was well lit, with tables and chairs scattered around, a piano in the corner, comfortable sofas and a large, full bookcase. It would be much easier to sew here than perched on a chair in the tiny cabin with just the one dim light. Bree asked directions to her cabin, fetched the bundle of clothing to be altered and returned to the common room. She chose a table in the corner and set to work.

Not long after, several male employees noticed her and came over to introduce themselves. Bree was polite, but firm. With the hours of work ahead of her, she had no time to spare parrying extravagant compliments and listening as they touted their various virtues. It took repeated pleas to be left alone, and a promise to visit with them another night, to get them to leave.

As evening aged into night, the room filled with more off-duty employees. The noise level increased, especially after a middle-aged man sat at the piano and played a series of Irving Berlin songs, including *Alexander's Rag Time Band*. Lady Rothberry's nephew had pounded out Mr. Berlin's music with gusto the past winter before the grande dame locked the piano.

Tables and chairs were cleared from a large area in the middle of the room and several people paired up and trooped out to dance. A trio of couples showed off their skills at the fox trot, and an amused chuckle burbled from her throat. "*A shìorraidh!*" Bree stuck herself again with the needle. She sucked on the injured digit, shaking her head at the dancer's enthusiastic gyrations. When the modern dances became popular up back home, Lady Rothberry had expressed her disapproval in no uncertain terms, complaining bitterly and often, stating the waltz was the only proper dance for genteel women.

Before she bent back to her sewing, a handsome black pair took the floor and danced a sultry tango. Bree couldn't take her eyes off them as they moved sensuously across the room, and she knew her face flamed by the time the dance ended. She cleared her throat and quickly turned back to her stitches.

It was late and the room was empty by the time Bree stood and stretched her cramped muscles. She gathered the completed garments and tools and went in search of her cabin. Anne's sleeping form occupied the lower bunk when Bree crept in. The dim light still burned, and she made a mental note to thank her roommate for being so thoughtful. She struggled to make her bed with as little noise as possible, wishing she'd had the foresight to do it earlier after cracking her head on the low ceiling several times. Bree crawled from corner to corner tucking in the sheets, an unsatisfactory method resulting in wrinkled sheets that probably wouldn't stay where they belonged.

After she dug her nightgown out of the wardrobe as quietly as possible, she wearily climbed the ladder. She pulled the coarse sheets and scratchy blanket up to her chin and got comfortable, then realized with a groan that she'd forgotten to turn out the light. Her jaws popped with a huge yawn, and she decided it wouldn't hurt to leave it on. Bree closed her eyes, her mind roiling with the fantastic changes this momentous day brought to her life. "What on earth will tomorrow bring?" she wondered, as sleep overtook her.

Chapter 3

Friday, April 12 through Saturday, April 13

A loud bang on the door shocked Bree awake. Anne moaned as she stumbled out of bed below. Bree sat up, catching herself just in time to prevent another headache. Anne looked up and smiled as she ran fingers through her tousled blonde hair.

"Mornin', Bree. As soon as we're dressed, I'll show you the best dining room. We can have breakfast together. Since I'm assigned to second class, we won't see much of each other during the day. I tried to wait up for you last night but it got so late, and we have to get up early."

Bree waved off the apology. "I'm glad you didn't. I found a nice cozy spot in an employee lounge and stayed up to alter my uniforms. By the way, thanks for leaving the light on for me," she said as she climbed down the ladder.

"No problem. I'm so tired by the time I hit the pillow, it could be broad daylight and it wouldn't bother me." She opened the wardrobe and pulled out a fresh uniform. "You must have found the big common room. I went there the first night, but ended up staying out dancing so late I almost didn't make my shift in the morning. I decided I'd better stay away. There's another, smaller, lounge up near the bow. It's much quieter and they have a good library. I go there most nights for a while after dinner. It's not as much fun, but I don't want to risk getting into trouble. There's time enough for that when we get to New York, right?" Anne grinned and waggled her eyebrows, and Bree couldn't help but laugh.

The blonde pinned her watch to the top of her apron and exclaimed, "Oh, Lord, if we don't get a move on, we're going to be in trouble right now."

Bree finished tying the apron of her own uniform and they hustled out into the hallway. As they hiked the long corridors to the dining hall, Anne pointed out reference points to help Bree find her way around the ship on her own.

Breakfast was plentiful and of good quality, but Bree worried so much about being late to work she only managed a few bites before she scurried off. Her reward was a lengthy wait outside the tailoring room. When Mr. Thorpe eventually showed up, he merely sniffed in greeting before he unlocked the door and led the way in.

Bree returned the tools she'd borrowed. He showed her where and how each piece should be kept. The tailor shop was extremely well organized, with a special nook or cranny for everything. She set to work on a replenished pile of clothing that repeated the prior day's contents of buttons, lace and mending. Mr. Thorpe seemed to spend most of his time puttering around the room as he rearranged papers and checked her work. Conversation was minimal.

Bree enjoyed a brief respite at noon for a quick meal in a different, smaller employee dining room. Because she didn't know anyone, she avoided entering any of the animated conversations eddying around her. With only thirty minutes to eat, she knew it would be difficult to get to know anyone, so she didn't linger.

The afternoon passed slowly as Bree worked her way through the seemingly endless pile of mending. At six o'clock precisely, Mr. Thorpe cleared his throat and stood, giving her a slight inclination of his head toward the door. Bree quickly put away the few tools she'd gathered during the day and hurried out into the corridor. She headed to her cabin, leaving Mr. Thorpe locking the door.

As she set foot on the lower stair up to E Deck, she couldn't help but reflect on her previous encounter with the boorish young man. She grudgingly admitted, boorish or not, it was impossible to keep from scanning the hallway each time she passed, secretly hoping to see him again. "And I'm a foolish *Cailín*, I am. He's rude and forward, and like as not would get me into a pickle with Mr. Thorpe or Mr. Barton," she muttered.

Back in her cabin, she removed her wrinkled uniform, hung it carefully in the closet, and donned one of her own outfits. As she washed her face in preparation for dinner, Bree tried, not very successfully, to forget dancing cobalt eyes.

Anne breezed through the door and smiled. "Oh, I'm so glad you're here. We can have dinner together and I can show you around some more."

Bree was happy to have someone to talk to after the near silence of her day, and Anne provided a much-needed distraction. The blonde had made numerous friends in the first few days of the cruise and introduced Bree to everyone she knew in the dining room and, later, in the small forward lounge. Bree finally gave up trying to keep names and faces straight and just focused on memorizing directions to the various employee gathering places and identifying the areas people worked in by the type of uniform they wore.

They called it an early night and climbed wearily into their bunks.

* * * *

The next day began as a repeat of the previous one, with the exception of waking in the pitch black darkness of the cabin. Bree sighed thankfully when Anne managed to slap the light switch on her third try. She found it disconcerting not to see her hand waving in front of her face without the dim fixture on the ceiling. A momentary jolt of fear flashed through her mind at the thought of being caught in the maze of dark corridors if the ship's lights were to somehow turn off. She shuddered.

Anne laughed at her fears and pointed out emergency lights. They went their separate ways after breakfast, agreeing to meet in the cabin when their shifts ended.

After work, Anne wheedled Bree into donning her second-best dress for a visit to the larger common room after dinner, pointing out there were only a few more days aboard ship to meet other employees. When Bree reminded her of her vow to stay out of trouble, Anne just laughed and said, "I didn't say we had to go to bed early *every* night! Come on, Bree. We'll have to stay in a rooming house in New York right by the docks. If we don't find someone who knows the city, we won't get to see any of it before we sail again. It'll be ever so much more fun if we have a local to show us around. Please, please, please?"

Bree finally gave in to her roommate's ardent pleas with a laugh, shaking her head ruefully.

* * * *

Seated in the packed dining hall, Bree gaped at the menu, amazed at the wide variety of dinner options allowed. She had her choice of fish, lamb, chicken or turkey--the same menu offered to second class passengers. For dessert, Bree tried American ice cream.

"This is the most wondrous thing I've ever tasted!" she declared as she licked the frozen concoction off her spoon after scraping the bottom of her bowl clean.

Anne countered, "It can't be as good as these coconut sandwiches!"

They still argued good-naturedly as they headed to the lounge. As on her first night aboard ship, the large room filled quickly. More singles and couples strolled into the room until all the tables, sofas and chairs were filled to overflowing. The same man plopped down at the piano amid clapping and hooting, and pounded out more raucous show tunes. Couples streamed out onto the dance floor.

Bree and Anne exchanged looks and giggled as a phalanx of young males headed toward their table and vied for dance partners. The rest of the evening became an exciting whirlwind of dancing,

31

laughing, and fending off more than a few eager advances. Anne kept reassuring an inexperienced Bree the evening was perfectly normal for young, single females in the company of young, single males. Pulled, yet again, onto the dance floor by an Italian first class steward, Bree laughed out loud, amazed at how much fun she was having.

They danced late into the night. Bree, completely tuckered out, had to drag Anne back to their cabin, amid sighs and entreaties for "just one more dance" from the group of zealous partners they left behind.

Bridget fell asleep as soon as she snuggled down into her hard mattress.

* * * *

Malcolm wandered the shadowed deck, breathing in the salt-tinged air. The sound of chamber music from The Parisian Restaurant drifted on the wind. He wore a heavy wool coat, collar turned up against the chill. The temperature had plummeted when the sun went down and few other passengers braved the open promenade.

He'd been making the rounds of all the public rooms for the past two days, searching for a jaunty tangle of coppery hair. So far, his efforts were for naught. It seemed quite strange he hadn't been able to find even one person who recognized his description of Miss Barry, or who had heard of her. Malcolm shivered as he rounded a protective bulkhead and caught the stiff breeze full in his face. He decided to give up the hunt for the night and resume on the morrow.

Chapter 4

Sunday, April 14

Bree felt like she'd only just crawled into bed when she awoke to the annoying pounding on the door. She had to rouse a gently snoring Anne and physically push her out the door for their morning ablutions. After she downed a second cup of strong coffee, her roommate responded to conversation without constant yawns. They parted after a quick breakfast and a few minutes later Bree stepped off the last tread to F Deck.

Before she schooled her mind against it, she found herself surveying the empty corridors. As she headed toward the tiny workroom, she muttered under her breath about being spellbound by Asrais, the water faerie that like to cause trouble aboard ships. An odd thumping drew her attention, and she noted a sign that said *Squash Court*. The vision of gourds arguing law on a ship sent her into a peal of laughter as she hurried down the hall. She barely managed to get her mirth under control before entering Mr. Thorpe's lair. Moments later, she was ensconced on the hard chair, surrounded

33

by a new pile of mending. Her boss spent his time slowly opening and closing seemingly random drawers at his desk.

The hallway door had been left open to ventilate the stuffy room and, at midmorning, a steward appeared. He silently handed Mr. Thorpe a note. The old man clucked his tongue over the contents of the message before he turned to Bree.

"One of the first class passengers requires our services. You will follow this man to their cabin and see what is needed. Often our customers wish you to do the sewing there. If you are unable to do so, or they prefer, bring the garments here and complete the work. Speak as little as possible, be extremely polite and do not, under any circumstances, argue. I'd better not hear about any problems, understand?"

Bree bobbed her head, knowing it was no use telling him she knew how to behave.

Mr. Thorpe handed her a heavy wooden box with a leather handle on top. "This is your kit. Make sure you bring it back intact. The cost of anything missing will be deducted from your wages."

Bree took time to open it, knowing she risked his wrath, but wanting to make sure it included everything she would need. The interior was ingenious, with oak trays on brass hinges that allowed them to swing up and away, revealing more trays below. There were spools of silk thread in dozens of colors, cards of needles and packets of long pins. Two pairs of sharp scissors, one large and one small, fit into felt-lined shallow trays. Folding measuring sticks, thimbles and a jar of assorted buttons completed the contents. The head tailor might be unfriendly, but he clearly did know his business.

Before Bree investigated further, Mr. Thorpe cleared his throat. She quickly replaced the trays, latched the box and turned to the steward. As Bree stepped out into the corridor, the tailor called out, "Remember what I said, young lady, and don't dawdle on your way back here. We have lots of work and can't afford time wasted on idle chit-chat with everyone you come across."

She didn't bother answering, too busy scurrying along to catch up with the fast-moving steward. Bree followed his stiff, black-clad figure up five levels of service stairs to A Deck, then down a hallway and out onto the open polished teakwood deck. She realized they were in the forward first class section. It was difficult to keep up, and several times she nearly collided with furniture or people as her inquisitive gaze was drawn by the sight of gentlemen in lounge coats escorting women in colorful frocks with large-brimmed, fanciful hats and parasols. Children in sailor suits and knee britches or frilly white dresses followed in their wake, herded by frazzled nannies. Bree trotted along behind the steward, who kept up a brisk pace, weaving between the passengers. He turned back inside the ship, went a short distance down a plush carpeted and paneled hall and stopped outside a carved wooden door with a shiny brass *Suite A5* plaque. He knocked.

The door was opened by a frail woman in a quilted dressing gown, her blue-veined hand grasping the collar tight to her neck. The steward bowed. "Madame, this is the seamstress, Miss Barry. She will assist you. Is there anything else you require at this time?"

The woman shook her head slightly, her face pale and tense, eyes red-rimmed. "No, thank you, Mr. Cave. I believe you've taken quite good care of me for the moment." Her voice was so low Bree barely caught the words.

"Very good, madam."

The steward bowed again and slipped away, striding down the corridor. Bree turned to find the woman observing her closely.

"Come in, my dear." She stepped back and motioned Bree in. "I'm Elizabeth. I'm afraid I've left this until the last moment. I'm not sure you can help me." She led the way through a large sitting room into an equally large bedroom. On the bed lay a beautiful gown in the popular new Oriental design. Emerald green silk shimmered with elaborate gold embroidery of storks, windswept hillsides and cherry blossoms. Handkerchief folds of embroidered tulle draped from the high waist. The dress had narrow shoulder straps and tiny pleats across the bosom with a low, straight neckline.

"You see, I seem to have lost some weight, and now this dress is simply hideous on me. My husband particularly insisted I wear the gown to dinner tonight at the captain's table. My dear friends, the Astors, will be attending, and Eldon will be quite put out if I show up 'looking like a half-starved old crone', as he so eloquently described it." She wrung her hands and peered over her shoulder as if she expected her angry husband to arrive at any moment. "On top of that, I'm afraid I don't have a maid to help me dress. I realize it's a great deal to ask, but if you could perhaps fit the dress a bit and assist me to get ready tonight, I would appreciate it ever so much."

36

"I'm sure we can manage, ma'am. I'll just help you slip the dress on so I can see what needs to be done."

As the woman removed her wrapper, Bree gathered the voluminous silk skirt up and turned to drop it over the taller woman's white-blonde head. Through the sheer fabric of the woman's shift Bree saw an extensive bruise covering the woman's entire side, from armpit to thigh, colored in deep purple, red and yellow. She gasped. "*A Thighearna*! Whatever happened? That must hurt *uafàsach*!" She realized she'd lapsed into Gaelic in her concern when the woman gave her a confused glance. "Horribly. It must hurt horribly!"

Elizabeth looked away. "I'm so clumsy, you see. I fell. I hit...er...the edge of the bathtub. It does hurt quite dreadfully. I knew I wouldn't be able to manage this by myself."

Bree frowned. "You should be in bed." She bent down and inspected the brilliantly colored bruise. "*Dhuine*! Didn't your husband hear you cry out?"

Elizabeth wouldn't meet her eye. "No. No, he wasn't here. He left before it happened," she said in a dead voice.

Bree felt sick to her stomach, afraid she really *did* see. Not again. "I think you need a doctor. I'm sure you've broken a rib or two and they could do a great deal of damage if not taken care of. Let me see if Mr. Cave is nearby and I'll have him fetch the ship's doctor." She laid the dress on the bed and started to turn away.

"No," Elizabeth said firmly. "I won't have a stranger poking and prodding at me. I'll be fine. Let's get the dress fitted. I don't want to be late tonight. It would so distress Eldon."

37

"Ma'am, you won't be all right. I've seen something like this before. It will be very painful every time you move, and if the rib is broken, you might cause further damage. You must have it wrapped." Bree knew what might happen and refused to stand by and watch the gentle woman go through it.

Elizabeth's shoulders slumped. "Oh, very well but not the ship's doctor. There is a woman I met, she seems ever so nice. She's a doctor. Her name is Alice. Alice Leader. Perhaps if Mr. Cave found her?"

Bree dashed to the door and opened it. As luck would have it, the steward glided toward her with a pair of boots in his hand.

"Is there something the lady requires, miss?" he asked with a disapproving glower. Obviously, he thought Bree was getting above herself and expected him to cater to her.

Bree didn't waste time on the etiquette of servant classes. "Yes, sir. The lady needs a doctor."

His irritation immediately changed to concern. "What's happened? Has she taken ill?" He craned his neck to see past Bree.

"No, she took a bad fall earlier. I think she may have broken a rib or two. She refuses to see the ship's doctor, but she met a woman--a Doctor Leader. Do you know her?"

"Why, yes. She has a double with her husband just down the corridor. I'll see if she's there, and if she isn't, I'll find her straight away."

"Thank you, Mr. Cave." He gave her a look that might have indicated grudging respect, then turned and trotted off.

As he hurried away, Bree shut the door and went back to Elizabeth's side. "He knows the doctor and will fetch her. Please, won't you lie down?"

Elizabeth sighed and shook her head, wincing and cradling her ribs with crossed arms. "Oh, my. That does hurt."

"More than a bit, I'd wager." Bree helped the older woman perch carefully on a chair while they waited for the doctor.

"My mother was hurt, er, hurt herself, the same way, and the pain was terrible," Bree said. She couldn't bring herself to tell this sweet woman what had happened after her mother's "fall." She just knew she wouldn't sit quietly by and watch it all over again.

Since Elizabeth seemed determined to dress for dinner, Bree stepped into the suite's parlor, opened her kit and selected the thread and implements she would need to alter the dress. She spoke over her shoulder. "How long have you and your husband been married, if I'm not being impertinent?"

Elizabeth chuckled softly. "Of course not, my dear. We married three years ago. My first husband, Percy, died seven years ago. It was so sudden. One day he was fine, the next he was gone. Eldon is--was--Percy's older brother. He was such a godsend after Percy died. I don't know how I would have managed the business, and my son just off to university. He courted me quite enthusiastically, asking for my hand several times, but I wasn't ready for another man in my life. Then my business manager disappeared and took quite a lot of money with him. Eldon convinced me, and rightly so, I didn't have a head for business. I needed him to help me, if not for myself, then for my son. It was very inconvenient for him to have to keep running out to The Dell to help me or explain the intricacies of business. I was being quite unfair. It's much easier for him now."

Bree bit her tongue. Not a word about love--not for her or for him. It was just *easier*. Bree flashed on the sound of her own father's patronizing voice ridiculing her mother for thinking herself more capable of handling their financial affairs than he. Bree had never met Elizabeth's husband, but it sounded as if Bree's father could have been Eldon's brother instead of Percy. "What was Percy like? Were he and his brother similar?"

"Dear me, no. Percy was such a quiet, unassuming man. Kind and patient. He had a way about him. The workers adored him. He knew them all by name and asked about their families. Percy insisted I go with him when he visited the factories. He felt I needed to be involved in the business and planned to have our son take over one day. Eldon is very forceful and outspoken. He likes to 'wade right in' as he calls it, and take action without any assistance or interference from anyone else." She shifted on the chair and winced.

"Is your son with you on this trip to help you with the business?" Bree asked, in an attempt to distract Elizabeth from her injury.

"Oh, yes. He studied business at Harvard so he'd be prepared to handle the company, and he's quite brilliant."

Bree smiled at the motherly bias.

"He's twenty-five but Eldon says the board of directors doesn't think he has enough experience yet to take over the reins. That's why I invited Mal to the continent with us this year. Eldon wasn't very happy when he found out that I...well that is to say, when I felt up to discussing the details. He said it was to have been our time alone."

Bree knew what she meant was when she finally got up the nerve. "What business are you in?"

"Textiles and garments. The big mills are in Massachusetts and we have smaller ones in several other places. We manufacture ladies' fashions, mostly in New York. We started coming to Europe last year to attend the new fashion shows in France. Mal heard about them from some friends of his. Eldon wasn't sure at first, but it's been a wonderful idea."

The unknown term intrigued Bree. "What are fashion shows?"

"Several of the large couturiers in France have them. They present their newest designs in a large room. Young women wearing the costumes walk around so we can see how the gowns fit and drape. It's quite marvelous. It helps us know what fabrics and styles will be popular in Europe this year so we can plan our clothing designs for next year. It takes a year or so for the European designs to make their way across the ocean, you see. We manufacture ready-to-wear clothing, so of course our garments aren't so elaborate, but I've always believed every woman should be able to wear stylish clothes even if she can't afford French couture."

"It sounds to me like you know quite a lot about the business."

Elizabeth gave a tiny, deprecating wave. "Percy used to talk to me about things in the evenings over a glass of wine. Eldon is too busy. He has a great deal of meetings with buyers, and travels frequently to make sure our business expands. I often don't see him for days at a time."

"What are the styles this year?" Bree said, but a knock on the door interrupted her. She opened it to find Mr. Cave standing next to a tall, kindly-looking woman with a black leather bag in hand.

"This be Dr. Leader, miss." He bowed to the doctor and inclined his head to Bree before he headed down the corridor.

Bree quickly ushered Dr. Leader into the bedroom, and the woman went straight to Elizabeth. She knelt beside her and asked a series of questions, while she gently examined Elizabeth's side, back and stomach. After a thorough assessment, she pulled several lengths of linen from her bag and carefully wrapped the material around Elizabeth's torso, securing the end with a tiny barbed clip. She stood and said, "Let's get you to bed."

"Oh, I can't do that. Miss Barry is going to alter my gown and then I have to get ready for dinner with my husband."

An argument ensued as the doctor tried to talk Elizabeth out of her plans, but she relented when she realized Elizabeth's decision was firm. Turning to Bree, Dr. Leader said, "She mustn't move any more than absolutely necessary."

Bree nodded.

"Madam, if you insist on this foolish behavior, I can guarantee you'll be in constant pain." Dr. Leader reached into her bag. She held up a white envelope. "I'll give you some powdered laudanum, but I beg you not to stay out late, and don't have any alcohol. You shouldn't be alone after you take it, either. I don't know how you'll react. You might wake up disoriented and dizzy and end up causing

42

further damage."

"Well, Eldon certainly can't stay with me. He has several business meetings scheduled after dinner. I'll be fine."

Bree spoke up. "I could sit with you."

Elizabeth regarded her with grateful surprise. "You would do that, my dear? Oh, I am so sorry, I never even enquired as to your first name. Please forgive me."

Bree smiled away the apology. "My name is Bridget. Please, call me Bree. I haven't any plans tonight, and if you have other gowns you'd like altered, I could do them for you while I'm here."

"It's settled then," the doctor said as she snapped her bag shut. "Take a quarter teaspoon of powder in a glass of water right away. You may have another quarter teaspoon before bedtime if you need it, but not a pinch more."

Bree nodded and accepted the proffered envelope. She walked the doctor to the door where they paused.

"Under no circumstance should you leave her alone. Do you understand?"

Bree looked into Dr. Leader's sharp brown eyes and realized the woman had formed the same conclusion as she about how Elizabeth came to be hurt. "Yes, I do. May I call you if there are problems?"

"Certainly. Send the steward for me at any time. Good night."

Bree shut the door and went to the cabinet against the wall. She poured a draught of water from a pitcher into a cut-glass tumbler. She carefully measured out the prescribed amount of pain medicine, stirred it into the glass and took it in to Elizabeth, who drank it down without protest.

They sat talking about France for a quarter hour, until Elizabeth said she felt quite a bit better. After first making sure the pins and measuring stick were handy, Bree helped Elizabeth to her feet and gently tugged the gown into place.

The bodice gaped away from the woman's chest and the fabric fell in unbecoming folds to puddle on the floor, like a child playing dress-up. Clearly, she'd lost more than a little weight and was near to skin and bones.

With a nod and smile to reassure a fretful Elizabeth, Bree went to work. She pulled the straps up until the gown hung correctly and pinned them, then took up additional pleats across the bodice and sides until it fit snuggly. She quickly secured the hem and eased the dress off. Bree caught Elizabeth as she tottered, the older woman's elbow knocking Bree's cap askew. It fell to the floor and rolled under a side table as Bree led her to a velvet chaise.

"Thank you, dear. I do feel a bit dizzy," Elizabeth said, a hand on her brow.

"I think the doctor is right. You should stay in, though I know you'd hate to miss the dinner party."

"Oh, it's not that. I never really enjoy these dinners. Eldon insists everyone misses me if I don't attend, but many of the people at table are Eldon's friends or business acquaintances I've not met before. I dislike making small talk with strangers. It seems I'm always on the wrong side of politics, and rarely attend the theater so I don't know which plays are the current rage. Most of his friends aren't interested in books, but reading is the one thing I do a lot. It's Eldon everyone wants to see. He's very amusing and clever. And handsome. Some of the women, even married ones, are so forward with him I can't believe it. I really don't think anyone even notices if I'm sitting there or not."

Bree expelled the breath she hadn't realized she held. This was too familiar. Having escaped the atmosphere she'd grown up in, she was shocked to find it existed in the thin air of the elite as well. Her own mother, a gentlewoman, had been surrounded by her husband's coarse and often drunken friends--people with whom she had nothing in common. They had followed Bree's father's lead, making his wife miserable in every way possible.

Bree determined to help this time. "I guess we'll have to make you so lovely everyone, including Eldon, will be too busy staring to make silly small talk."

Elizabeth gazed down at her hands and sighed. "I don't know why Eldon married me. I'm lucky he even noticed me with all the beautiful women who flutter around him. I'm so boring and he's so exciting. He has everyone on the edge of their seats, waiting for his next word."

Bree looked closely. The older woman had a great beauty under the lines of sadness. Only a few faint streaks of gray showed in the fine, white-blonde hair. Elizabeth's huge gray eyes were deeply sunken above sculpted cheekbones, her skin flawless. A straight nose perched above wide, full lips. Her graceful neck had yet to show folds of loose skin. Her type of beauty only improved with age.

45

Bree knew she was a total opposite with her mop of auburn hair and spattering of faint freckles, which proclaimed her Irish ancestry.

"We'll just see about that," she said. "When we get done, he'll have eyes for no one but you." Bree hadn't been able to help her own mother. If she aided this woman, perhaps it would help make up for it in some way.

Time slipped away. After assisting Elizabeth to lie down until it was time to dress, Bree set about altering the gown. She worked feverishly, her fingers flying over the fabric. The big round windows were just beginning to show stars as, with a heavy sigh of relief, Bree tugged a thread to tighten the final knot and clipped the silk with her scissors. She quickly took a few measurements to help her with alterations on the other gowns and laid the dress over her arm. From the bedroom doorway, she peeked in and found Elizabeth awake, her expression dreamy.

"Is it done already? I almost hoped it wouldn't be, but I suppose I mustn't disappoint Eldon."

"Does it matter so much, ma'am?" Bree asked.

Elizabeth nodded and struggled out of bed. Bree hurried to help her. As Bree held the dress up, the older woman seemed to shrink within herself, then sighed and removed her robe. Bree carefully slipped the dress over her head and did up the line of frog fasteners at the back. She helped Elizabeth into the matching emerald green heeled shoes with jeweled buckles and they stepped over to the large standing mirror.

Elizabeth's gray eyes widened in shock. Where before the dress had made a mockery of her figure, it now enhanced her slight curves. The tucked bodice pushed her bosom up to show creamy cleavage above the neckline. Billowing fabric fell in graceful folds to skim the floor, the toes of her shoes peeping out.

"Oh, my!" was all Elizabeth said.

Bree gently urged her over to the dressing table and pulled the woman's long hair from the loose knot at the base of her neck. With a sterling-handled brush, she smoothed the flaxen hair back from her high forehead and pulled it into a sleek chignon. She slid in diamond-encrusted combs, which had been lying casually on the table. As she admired the effect in the mirror, Bree considered the simple, elegant style more becoming for Elizabeth's fine, straight hair than the currently popular Gibson up-do.

"Have you any other jewelry to wear?"

"The blue case." Elizabeth gestured to a large, carved burlwood box.

Bree lifted the lid and pulled out a thin enameled case. She flipped it open and gasped at the glistening necklace and matching earrings nestled on white satin. "They're beautiful. Just like you."

Elizabeth tittered softly as she clipped the earrings on and Bree fastened the necklace's lobster-claw clasp. A triple strand of pearls interspersed with teardrop emeralds and diamonds glowed above the shimmering green silk. The large table-cut emerald pendant ringed by shimmering diamonds and emerald hung heavily between the swell of her breasts. Their eyes met in the dressing table mirror. Elizabeth smiled shyly and Bree was gratified by the astonished happiness on the older woman's face.

"Now, are you ready to show off at the captain's table?"

"Oh, yes. Eldon will be so pleased." She carefully turned and clasped Bree's hands. "Thank you so much. I never thought..." Her eyes brimmed with tears.

"Here, now. None of that. Don't go spoil the effect with red, puffy eyes."

Elizabeth dabbed the tears away with an embroidered handkerchief and pushed herself upright with the help of the tabletop and Bree's assistance. "Oh dear. Look at the time. Eldon will be here any moment." Her brow creased as the woman lapsed into fear of not meeting her husband's expectations--the same expression she'd seen on her mother's face countless times. Bree thought of several appropriate Gaelic curses she'd like to apply to Elizabeth's husband, but kept her silence.

Instead, she said, "What wrap would you like to wear? It will be chilly on deck." Bree walked to the large armoire and opened it. A bounty of fabrics and colors spilled out, and a section of furs filled the corner. A long-haired gray fox matched Elizabeth's eyes and Bree pulled it out, seeing the older woman's fretting prevented her from making the decision on her own.

"This would be lovely with your eyes. And it has a matching muff--what fun! Now, what about a hat?" Bree chattered as Elizabeth watched her with a growing smile. Hatboxes lined the top of the armoire and, with the help of a side chair, Bree hauled them down one at a time. As she stepped down off the chair, she caught her heel in her apron hem and tore a section loose. Rather than risk tripping over it again, she slipped it off and folded it over the chair to mend later. In the third hatbox, she found a broad-brimmed hat with fox trim and fan of dyed gray feathers at the crown. Rosettes of gray satin circled the brim. She quickly fashioned tiny leaves using small pieces of green silk she'd trimmed when altering the gown, adding them to the rosettes. White opera-length gloves in a dressing table drawer completed the outfit.

As Bree put the finishing touches on the hat, the door banged open and a big, blustery man strode into the room. His ebony hair shone almost blue under the electric lights, distinguished white streaks running back from his temples.

"Well, if this isn't a sight." He looked intently at Elizabeth and the older woman held her breath as she waited for his comments. Surprise flickered across his features. He gave Elizabeth a tiny nod, just enough to bring a flush of happiness to his wife's face. "Have you found a new maid, my dear?" His voice was deep and mellow, but Bree didn't like it all the same.

"Eldon! You're early. We're almost finished," Elizabeth stammered. "This is Bree Barry. She's altering my gowns and helping me dress."

Eldon turned his back to his wife and Bree knew it was on purpose as he gave her a leer that sent shivers down her back. She had never been scrutinized in such a calculating manner, save perhaps by Lord Rothberry that last night.

"Since Eleanor took off and left you without a maid, I'm glad to

49

see you've found someone who can make you presentable. I dislike all the questions when you show up looking like death warmed over."

Elizabeth blushed and hung her head.

"I can't believe your wife could be anything but lovely, and with her injury, she wasn't able to dress by herself." Bree refused to keep silent. It was all she could do not to snap the words out.

Eldon shot her a penetrating glance then offered a smarmy smile. "Of course I didn't mean it like that. I've been very concerned since she became ill." He gave Elizabeth a long, warning stare. "Some days she can barely drag herself out of bed, and she's gotten rather clumsy as well. I'm happy to see her looking and feeling better. If you've had a hand, I must show you my appreciation in some way."

He hadn't commented on the injury. If he'd been unaware of it, surely he would have asked what happened and expressed some concern about her condition? Bree took a deep breath and bit back words she longed to say, murmuring instead, "There is no need. I am simply performing my duties, and as I said, enjoying it." She directed the last comment to Elizabeth. It seemed to raise the older woman's spirit and she lifted her head, smiling timidly.

"I'll be here when you return from dinner, ma'am. In the meantime, I'll go through your other dresses and see what I can do to fit them for you."

Elizabeth nodded distractedly, her attention centered on her husband's glowering face.

Someone knocked at the door. Eldon glared at the portal. Elizabeth seemed frozen in place. Bree hesitated then moved across the room, calling over her shoulder, "I'll get that," as she reached for the latch. She turned to face the door and jerked back. A fist hung in the air in front of her face. She stumbled and would have fallen, but the man who was in the process of knocking on the door lunged forward and captured her in a firm, but gentle, grasp.

"Pardon me, Miss Barry. It seems like I have a penchant for attempting to knock you off your feet. Of course, what I'd really like is to sweep you off your feet."

Bree's jaw dropped as she observed the same handsome man who'd nearly collided with her in the companionway. It dawned on her--Elizabeth's son, Mal. Malcolm DuMont. Elizabeth had never mentioned her last name. Bree studied his face, noting the slightly sardonic tilt of his eyebrows and hint of a smile. He was clearly a spoiled, rich rake, who thought pretty words would win over anything in a skirt. She closed her mouth with an audible snap. If he thought she would be his next conquest, he could just go to the devil.

Ignoring him, she turned to Elizabeth. "It appears you now have two escorts, ma'am."

"Malcolm, dear, I didn't expect to see you this evening." Elizabeth's gaze flicked uncertainly from her son's smiling face to her husband's frowning one.

"I decided to have dinner with you after all. And now I see how absolutely lovely you look tonight, I don't believe Eldon deserves to have you all to himself."

Elizabeth laughed gaily, but Bree saw Eldon's face darken as he directed a fierce glare at his stepson.

Malcolm moved to his mother's side and helped her into the fur coat. Over her shoulder he said, "And what about you, Miss Barry? Will you be joining us for dinner?"

Bree didn't hear any sign of sarcasm in his tone, but she knew, somehow, he was making her the butt of a joke. Surely he recognized her uniform? Then she remembered she wasn't wearing her cap or apron, only the plain dark dress.

Elizabeth gazed at her son in surprise as she slipped her hand into the fur muff. "Oh, yes. Of course." She turned to Bree and said kindly, "Would you like to join us, my dear?"

Of course the woman was trying to be polite and didn't expect to take her seamstress to dinner. Bree deliberately snubbed Malcolm and smiled at Elizabeth. "No, thank you, ma'am. I have a great deal to do tonight. I do hope you enjoy yourself."

Elizabeth pushed the muff high on one arm and took both Bree's hands in hers. "Thank you. You can't possibly know what this means to me."

Bree watched as Elizabeth, flanked by the two tall, muscular men, walked carefully into the hall. The door shut behind them.

She went to the wardrobe and pulled out a selection of gowns. Bree closed her eyes and leaned her forehead against carved wooden door and muttered, "Oh yes, I can, Mrs. DuMont. I know exactly how much it means to you. If only I could have given mother those same few moments of happiness." She sighed and went to work, knowing it would be late when she finished and she'd have little sleep before it was time to return to Mr. Thorpe's domain.

Chapter 5

Malcolm followed a few paces behind the older couple. Eldon perfunctorily offered his arm to his wife and, staring straight ahead, strode down the corridor. Elizabeth glanced up at him repeatedly, like a puppy hoping for words of praise from its master, as she scurried to keep up.

He frowned. Something was wrong. Mother walked very awkwardly, as if there were pebbles or something in her shoe. He knew from experience she wouldn't complain, especially to Eldon. He'd have to get her alone to find out what the matter was.

They proceeded down the hall and out onto the deck. Malcolm watched as Eldon regally greeted select passengers along the way, cutting those he considered beneath his station. After they reentered the ship, they turned down the massive curved staircase and joined the jumble of elegantly dressed passengers in the reception room. While waiting their turn to enter the dining salon, Malcolm noted the flooring. It looked like marble, but he'd been told it was a new material, quite *en vogue*, called *Linoleum*, rumored to be much more expensive than imported stone. They moved to the head of the line and were ushered into the brightly lit room by the prim maitre d'. Malcolm recognized several faces scattered throughout the hundred-foot-long expanse.

Eldon steered Elizabeth over to the captain's table. The men stood, including the distinguished Captain Smith, who smiled broadly, gave a stiff bow and clicked the heels of his highly polished shoes before he pulled out an empty chair on his right for Elizabeth. John Astor politely introduced Malcolm to the bearded and mustached captain, who wore his trademark long, black uniform with brass buttons, gold braided cuffs, and medals on his left breast.

Since the table was full with the addition of Eldon and his mother, Malcolm asked a passing waiter to arrange for a table to be set up nearby. The flustered waiter checked with the captain, who gave a brief nod. The maitre d' hovered as a crew brought in a small table and chair and efficiently set up the place setting.

Malcolm perused the captain's table. His mother was unusually pale, but she smiled happily. The male guests were drawn like bees to a rose by her regal beauty. All except one. When Eldon caught Malcolm's gaze, his lip pulled up in a sneer and his narrowed eyes glinted malevolently. He turned to Elizabeth and put his arm around the back of her chair. The hair on the back of Malcolm's neck stood on end as he watched Eldon lean close to Elizabeth and say something. By all appearances, he was a loving husband whispering sweet nothings into his wife's ear, but almost instantly the happiness fled her face, replaced by a blank, stunned expression. She seemed to shrink into her chair. Eldon observed Malcolm's anger with a smug, self-satisfied smile.

Malcolm started out of his chair but a line of waiters cut in front of him and laid plates around the table, refilled beverages and took away salad plates. By the time they retreated, he heard his mother giving apologies for not feeling well and begging her husband's pardon. Malcolm immediately stood and moved around to help her as she struggled out of her chair.

Eldon turned back to his audience and was into one of his "amusing stories" before they were three feet from the table.

"Are you all right, Mother? Something is wrong. What happened?" he whispered.

"Oh, you know me. Just one of my 'spells' as Eldon calls them. I don't think I could manage dinner and conversation tonight. I'm sorry. You don't need to go back with me. I can find my way. Why don't you go on and find some of your friends? You don't need to fuss about your old mother. I'll just go on to bed. Bree will assist me."

"It's not one of your so-called spells, Mother. You're hurt, aren't you? What happened?" he repeated, unwilling to allow her to sweep yet another incident under the rug.

"Really, dear, it's nothing. I took a spill." She wouldn't meet his eye.

"All right, we'll pretend for a moment you're fine. But you haven't had anything to eat. You and I are going to stop in at the A La Carte Dining Room and have a bite, and you can tell me all about your 'spill'."

"That's not necessary, Malcolm, and Eldon will be furious. He was so angry after you booked the suite. He said it was a waste of money and we'd have been quite comfortable with singles. If he finds out we ate in the A La Carte and paid extra, he'll be very unhappy. We can go back to the dining room if you're hungry."

He gritted his teeth at her concern for Eldon's feelings, since her husband would most certainly have dismissed thoughts of his wife by now. "No, Mother. I'll pay for dinner. We don't get to spend much time together, and this late there probably won't be a lot of people there to interrupt us," Malcolm said, as he escorted her down the hall. "Besides, I'd like to hear about how you came to have Miss Barry in your room." Malcolm looped his mother's arm though his own and walked her down the corridor, slowing his pace to match her hesitant one. "How did you meet the young lady, Mother? Is she the daughter of a new friend of yours?"

Elizabeth peered up at her son. "Are you teasing me, Malcolm?"

He stopped and turned to her. "I met her a couple days ago, but we didn't get much of a chance to talk. I've been trying to find out more about her, but perhaps you've saved me the effort."

"But Malcolm, dear, Bree is a seamstress. She works for the shipping line. Where on earth did you meet her?"

"A seamstress? She didn't speak like a common servant." Malcolm shook his head in bemusement as he remembered the plain dress she'd been wearing in his mother's suite. He'd also met her below decks. He was thrown by the elegant outfit she'd been wearing then, as well as her refined manners. She certainly didn't resemble the other workers with whom he'd come in contact on the ship. "Are you sure?"

"I assure you she is a very skilled seamstress." Elizabeth replied.

Malcolm steered her toward the restaurant, one hand scrubbing through the short hair at his nape as he considered the implications.

Chapter 6

Bree jerked as the doorknob rattled, sinking into the chair with relief when Elizabeth entered. She was making a silent prayer of thanks Eldon wasn't with his wife when Malcolm stepped into the room behind her.

He was very solicitous with his mother, leading her gently over to the chaise and helping her sit. When he turned his face, Bree saw a brittle gleam in his eyes. Apparently he had at least some idea of what happened.

"Mother tells me you've offered to sit with her tonight."

"Yes. I've been working on some of her other gowns, and it's no bother to stay." Bree couldn't tear her gaze away from his stormy eyes. They were indigo dark and bore into her with unnerving intensity. He shook his head and broke the spell.

"She's a little fatigued. Do you think you could help her to bed?"

"Of course." Bree laid the garment she'd been working on aside and quickly went to Elizabeth.

"I'm sorry I'm such a bother, dear," Elizabeth said.

Bree shushed her with a shake of her head. "Don't fret about it. We'll just get you settled in and comfortable." After she closed the bedroom door and helped the older woman out of the heavy gown and into her nightclothes, she gently brushed Elizabeth's hair. Pain lines deepened around her mouth and Bree quickly finished plaiting the silvery-blonde hair and eased her into the narrow bed, tucking the bedding close around her thin body. She fetched a glass of water from the bathroom, measured out the bedtime dose of laudanum then watched as Elizabeth drank it down.

"Thank you, my dear." Elizabeth reached up and brushed her hand across Bree's cheek. "You've been a godsend."

Bree grasped the thin hand as she stood, giving it a squeeze before tucking it under the blanket. "Sleep well, Mrs. DuMont. I'll be just outside the door. If you need me, call out." By the time she reached the door, Elizabeth's eyes were closed, her face unlined and peaceful in sleep. She left the door open a few inches and went back to her chair. Malcolm paced the room, his agitation palpable.

"She's resting now. The doctor gave her something to help the pain. I think she'll sleep for several hours," Bree said, avidly watching his long fingers scrub through glossy curls at the nape of his neck.

Malcolm's shoulders slumped and he closed his eyes, but Bree saw a muscle ticking in his jaw and knew anger seethed just beneath the surface. If he knew how his mother was injured, Eldon likely wouldn't enjoy their next meeting.

Malcolm confirmed her deduction as he issued a muffled oath, followed by detailed descriptions of several rather violent things he intended to do to his stepfather when he got his hands on him. He stopped pacing and glanced over at her. He noticed her wide eyes and slack jaw and gave her a sheepish look.

"I beg your pardon, Miss Barry. I've let my emotions run amok. Thank you for helping Mother. She speaks very highly of you. It's been difficult since her maid quit before we left Southampton. I don't believe Mother was particularly fond of Eleanor, since Eldon hired her without giving Mother any input, but they did eventually get to know each other's habits and such. It's clear she already thinks a great deal of you."

Bree smiled and nodded her thanks. Her smile faltered as Malcolm's deep blue eyes grew more intense, as though trying to read her thoughts. She quickly bent her head and focused on the dress in her lap. Should she comment on Elizabeth's injuries? It really wasn't her place. She wanted him to keep talking. She liked listening to his voice, liked having him near, even though it caused her to breathe too quickly. She didn't want him to notice, to wonder what it meant.

A muffled thump from the hallway startled her. Bree's gaze flicked to the door. The thought of Eldon walking in caused her heart to skip a beat. When the portal remained closed, she sucked in a breath and relaxed. As difficult as she found it to ignore the fact she was alone with Malcolm, she much preferred it to the prospect of being alone with Eldon.

"I hope you don't mind," he said, "but I think I'll stay a bit longer, to make sure Mother's sleeping comfortably."

Bree scrutinized Malcolm's expression, searching for a hint of his intentions. He stood in the middle of the room, feet apart, hands on hips, like a Greek god from the mythology lessons that had been part of her education at the Rothberrys. The sight gave her a strange flutter in her belly...and lower. She bit her lip in consternation.

Malcolm noticed her stare and mistook its meaning. He motioned to the connecting door. "If you prefer, I can remove to Eldon's room. Somehow I don't think we'll be seeing him for the rest of the night. But if I do, that would be fine too."

Bree was torn. Having him close kept her on tenterhooks, and she was succumbing to a strong attraction despite her attempts to the contrary. She tried to convince herself it was just worry about being alone if Eldon returned that made her want Malcolm to stay, and nothing to do with how he made her insides feel all fluttery and warm.

He was well within his rights to stay near his mother. Besides, they weren't technically alone together. It would be quite proper. Bree managed a casual shrug and said, "Why would I mind? I certainly understand your wanting to be near you mother."

He grinned at her, deep dimples bracketing his perfect smile. The sudden transformation was devastating. She felt her heart stop, or maybe it just truly started for the first time. Bree sucked air into her lungs. She'd forgotten to breathe for a long moment as she stared. Malcolm tilted his head and gave her an assessing look. She realized with an embarrassed start that her hungry gaze had gone on far too long. She swallowed and quickly turned to her sewing. Malcolm further tested her composure when he made himself comfortable on the sofa directly across from her.

He tucked a pillow into the small of his back, wriggling until satisfied with the fit. "Since we're going to spend the evening together, we should get to know one another better. Tell me about yourself, Miss Barry."

Bree slowly raised her eyes and she saw his benign expression of polite curiosity. She gnawed the inside of her lip. "There's not much to tell, really. I was born and raised in Queensland. I have seven brothers--" She paused at a gasp from the sofa.

"Seven brothers? My word, that doesn't seem very fair." Malcolm's eyes sparkled as his mouth curled into another devastating grin. Her heart gave a hard hiccup.

She took a shuddering breath and managed a small smile of her own. "No, actually, it wasn't very fair. We lived in a cottage on the Rothberry estate. My father's family has been gamekeepers there for several generations. My mother was the mayor's daughter, but when he died suddenly and left her destitute, she became a maid at the manor. She married my father just before the old lord died. His eldest son, the new lord, brought his wife to live at the manor, and she had my mother trained as a seamstress. When mother took sickly..." Bree paused and cleared her throat. "When mother took sick, I would go with her and help. She taught me everything about her work. She was a very good seamstress. After she died, I took her place at the manor." Bree looked down at her hands, clasped so tightly around the fabric she feared she'd never get the wrinkles out.

"How did you come to be on the ship? Is your family emigrating?" Malcolm asked.

"No. I left on my own." Bree kept her gaze averted as she smoothed the gown across her lap. She couldn't see his face. She feared if she did she might see he really wasn't interested, just making idle conversation. As long as she didn't know for sure, Bree could pretend he really wanted to know about her.

"How old are you, Miss Barry?" Malcolm chuckled at her affronted gasp. "I know that's quite an improper question, but you don't appear old enough to be on your own."

Bree sighed. How had she ended up in this most unusual conversation with him, anyway? She should stop it right now. Send him off to the other room so she had some peace and quiet. But she didn't like the idea of him thinking her a child, so she answered, "I'm nearly nineteen. Plenty old enough, thank you very much."

"Really?"

She heard genuine shock in his voice and looked up with a frown.

He must have realized how he sounded and gave her an apologetic shrug. "Well, be that as it may, being on your own in America is a tough proposition. Or do you intend to stay with White Star and travel the world?"

Bree tipped her head back and stared at the figured tin ceiling. She hadn't expected to be hired by the cruise line when she left home; she'd just wanted to get as far away from her family and the Rothberrys as possible. It had never occurred to her she could live on the seas and see exotic ports of call. She looked at Malcolm with a smile, "Now there's an idea. Maybe I will."

"With a boy in every port?" A devilish grin lit his eyes and deepened the dimples.

Bree couldn't help but laugh. "You never know."

As Malcolm opened his mouth to respond, a knock sounded at the door. Bree tensed, glad Malcolm was near. He stood and called, "Come in." Mr. Cave entered with a wheeled trolley. Bree sagged back into her seat.

"Here you are, sir. You didn't mention how many were dining or any particular preferences, so I took the liberty of making a selection for a light repast, along with coffee and tea."

Malcolm stepped to the cart and lifted silver domes off several plates to reveal fruit, cheeses, fancy iced petit fours and fat golden biscuits with jam and honey. "Thank you, Cave. This is more than adequate."

The steward gave a brief bow. "At your service, sir." He made a crisp turn and let himself out.

"I figured you might be hungry, Miss Barry. Mother and I had dinner, but you were left on your own."

Bree stared at him in surprise. "This is for me? Why, I couldn't eat all that."

"He *was* quite zealous in his selection." He smiled down at her. "Come now, take a break from your labor and have a bite. Mother would never forgive me if she thought you were being mistreated." He picked up a small frosted cake and bit into it. A fleck of icing at the corner of his expressive mouth captured her attention and she had to stop herself from licking her lips.

Bree's stomach rumbled loudly and she blushed. "Well, as you put it that way, I suppose I could eat something." She reached for a biscuit. From beneath lowered eyelids she hazarded a glance at Malcolm. His heavy-lidded eyes were half-closed, but the sparkle of blue revealed he observed her closely. She blushed deeper and looked away, silently cursing her fair skin.

He laughed softly and plopped back down on the sofa. She felt him watching as she made additional selections and poured herself a cup of tea. She used the china plate to nudge the sewing kit over and set her cup and saucer on the small side table. His intent scrutiny ruined her appetite.

As if he read her mind, he leaned back, tipped his head to the ceiling and perused the intricate patterns just as she had.

Bree's gaze focused on the tanned cords that ran up the sides of his neck. She noticed a sable curl wrapped around his right earlobe, cradling it. She yearned to reach out and touch it but picked up the cup of tea and saucer instead, taking a sip to wet her suddenly dry mouth.

"The steward will return shortly with linens to make up the sofa. If you prefer, I'll take the sofa and you may use the other bedroom."

Her cup rattled against the saucer and sloshed tea over the side. "I'd prefer the sofa, thank you, Mr. DuMont." She set the drink down as she tried to exorcize thoughts of occupying the big bed with Malcolm from her mind before she made a complete fool of herself.

"Enough of the 'Mr. DuMont,' please. My name is Malcolm, or Mal if you prefer. Mr. DuMont is far too formal for our circumstances. Besides, it makes me think of Eldon and I really don't care to think about him right now."

Bree nodded. "As you wish, Malcolm. You may call me Bridget."

"I thought I heard Mother call you Bree?"

"Well, yes. That's what my friends and family call me," she replied.

He laughed. "And *I* am not to call you Bree, I take it?"

She couldn't help the impish smile that turned up the corners of her mouth. "Not at this time."

He snorted, giving her the distinct feeling he wouldn't tolerate her mandate for very long.

Mr. Cave returned shortly with the linens. Malcolm stood to allow him to turn the sofa into a bed. After the steward left, Malcolm began pacing again. Bree watched, thinking of a tiger she'd seen once in a circus cage. They both showed the same sinewy grace and single-minded intent.

He halted and she dropped her gaze before he caught her staring. "I'll return shortly, Miss Barry. I think I'll see if I can find my stepfather and let him know of the new arrangements. I'll ask the steward to keep a close eye on the suite. I don't like to think about you and Mother being on your own here."

Before she responded, Malcolm strode purposefully out of the room then paused with the door half closed. "Lock the door behind me Bree, and the one to the adjoining room as well, if you please."

She nodded somberly, not wanting to read too much into his concern.

She flipped the latch behind him then did the same to the door into Eldon's chamber. The sudden silence in the suite became oppressive and Bree experienced a twinge of disappointment she would no longer be sparring with Malcolm. She knew it would be more restful without him watching her every move with those magnetic eyes, but still...

As she flounced into the chair and took up her sewing, her lips curled in a fiendish grin as she considered what might happen to Eldon if Malcolm caught up with him while in a temper. Eldon was a big man, but going to fat, while Malcolm was just as big and didn't appear to have a soft spot on him. Not in those broad shoulders, or narrow waist, or long legs. She chastised herself. It wasn't the least bit proper for her to have such intimate thoughts about a man she'd met only a few days ago. Oh, but he was quite a magnificent specimen of manhood!

* * * *

The clock on the mantle chimed half-past eleven, startling Bree. She glanced up in surprise. Surely it couldn't be so late? With dismay, she realized she'd never sent word to Mr. Thorpe that she would be staying to help Mrs. DuMont. It was too late now. "Oh, what if he fires me?" she moaned. Her vivid imagination conjured up several different scenarios, from being put off the ship on a desert island, to being sent to work in the bowels of the ship shoveling coal, to the unlikely event Mr. Thorpe would smile and say it was just fine, so long as she made the passenger happy. Unable to keep her mind on the gown she was working with, she stood and stretched, wincing as her stiff shoulder muscles popped. She rolled her neck and let her head hang, thoroughly exhausted and depressed.

A muted rumble and a vibration lasting several seconds brought her head up with a snap but the sounds weren't repeated. Bree wandered around the room aimlessly as she worked the kinks out of her back. With a heavy sigh, she picked up the gown again and prepared to get back to work. A loud thumping began at the door.

The normally composed voice of Mr. Cave shook with emotion. "Miss Barry? Miss Barry, please come to the door. It's urgent."

Chapter 7

Worried something had happened between Malcolm and Eldon, Bree raced to the door and frantically undid the lock.

The steward stood outside the door, perfectly groomed, as usual. His voice, however, was pitched higher than normal and his words even more clipped. "Please, miss, get the madam dressed in warm clothes. And get your life jackets."

"What is it? What's wrong?" Bree knew it would take something very serious indeed to cause him to expect an injured passenger to get out of bed.

He motioned her into the cabin and closed the door. He glanced toward the bedroom door and leaned in close to Bree's ear. "We've hit an iceberg, miss."

Bree protested, "Surely that's not a catastrophe. The *Titanic* is unsinkable."

"Not unsinkable, miss. No ship is unsinkable. I spoke with Mr. Ismay himself. He and Mr. Andrews have been speaking with the engineers, and the ship is sure to go down. Please, miss. Hurry.

They'll be loading the lifeboats very soon. I'll be back in a few moments to help you with the madam."

He turned and slipped out the door. Bree stood in the middle of the room and tried to decide whether she'd imagined the whole conversation. She became aware of loud voices in the corridor. She opened the door a few inches and was shocked to see passengers streaming into the hallway, some fully dressed and others in their nightclothes. Most carried life vests.

A stately older man held both his wife's hands in his, his other arm pulling her close as he spoke soothing words to her. A nearly hysterical woman carried a baby, a sleepy toddler stumbling along behind, calling out frantically, "Mrs. Forth, Mrs. Forth, I have the children!" Uniformed stewards moved through the crowd, urging them to put on their vests and proceed calmly. Bree slammed the door and leaned back against it. *Sinking!* She shook her head and tried to pull herself together. She rushed to Elizabeth's bedroom and called her name loudly. The woman moaned and rolled her head from side to side. Bree picked up her hand and lightly slapped the back of it, repeatedly commanding Mrs. DuMont wake.

Eyelids flickering, Elizabeth frowned sleepily and mumbled, "What is it, dear? Please don't shout."

"I'm sorry, Mrs. DuMont, but it's an emergency." The blonde head twisted toward the door. Bree reassured her, "It's not Eldon. The ship has struck an iceberg and it may sink. We don't have much time. We need to get you into some warm clothes and get your life vest."

"But, Bree, dear, the ship can't sink. It was in all the papers." Elizabeth blinked and tried to push herself upright. Bree slipped an arm behind her and eased her to a seated position.

"I'm sorry, Mrs. DuMont, but Mr. Cave assured me it's true. We don't have much time. Sit here for a moment and I'll gather up some clothing and a coat." She rushed to the armoire and found a heavy wool traveling suit then grabbed the thickest fur coat she found. Not bothering with the hatboxes, she rummaged through the lingerie cabinet and found a feather-soft wool scarf and fur-lined gloves.

It seemed to take an hour to dress Elizabeth. Tears ran down the elder woman's face, but she didn't complain. At last, all that remained was to slip on the heavy fur, wrap the scarf around her head and pull on the gloves. "Bree, dear, what about you?"

Bree looked down and realized her thin wool dress would provide minimal protection from the frigid air. "I'll run down and get my coat." But even as she spoke she heard more people moving down the corridor. She would have to fight her way through the crowd to the stairs, then get down four decks and back up again. She bit her lip as she debated what to do.

"Don't be silly, child. Take some of my clothing. I have more coats and gloves than I need, anyway. Why, we should see if anyone else needs anything."

Bree smiled at Elizabeth's kind suggestion. "What a wonderful idea." She ran to the armoire and pulled all the heavy fur and wool coats out then did the same with the scarves and gloves. She quickly selected items for herself then opened the door. The crowd had thinned considerably, and most of the people hurrying by appeared to be from second class or steerage. An older woman, who wore nothing but a cotton nightgown and a pair of men's boots, shuffled by. Bree ran out and threw a mink coat over her. The woman gaped at her, then pulled it close and scurried down the corridor, darting glances back. Bree quickly handed the remaining articles of clothing to those who looked most in need and turned to Elizabeth.

"Mr. Cave said he'd come back for us, but it's been quite a long time. Perhaps we should go on ahead?" Before Elizabeth responded, a quick knock sounded at the door. It opened to reveal the dapper steward, a white life vest strapped on over his uniform.

"You must put on your life jackets, ladies." He went into Eldon's bedroom and retrieved two bulky white jackets from the bottom of the armoire, staggering a bit.

Bree felt a slight tilt to the floor and realized the ship was actually beginning to list. Mr. Cave helped Elizabeth into her vest, while Bree, following his movements, put on her own.

"Quickly, now. The boat deck is already very crowded."

He led them through corridors and up a flight of stairs. Bree's ears were assailed as they stepped out into the night--sobbing women and children, the cries of crewmen trying to make sense of the chaos and shouts and curses from angry and frightened passengers. Hundreds of people pushed and shoved to get closer to the boats. The steward and Bree did their best to protect Elizabeth from the elbows and shoulders threatening to knock them all to the ground.

In a commanding voice, Mr. Cave jockeyed them to the front

lines. "Here, now, out of the way. Women and children first. You fellows, help make way for the ladies." Other women crowded in behind them as a narrow pathway opened.

Bree felt the tilt of the ship, and saw the lifeboats were beginning to swing away from the railing. Crewmen with ropes pulled the heavy wooden boats close as women and children climbed in. Four boats away several male passengers tried to climb into a boat and were driven back by the officers in a frightful melee, but not before one climbed the rail and jumped into the boat. Bree was shocked at the man's shameful behavior.

The steward managed to get them places in the nearest boat. Elizabeth, mouth clamped tight, bore her pain in silence as she was manhandled into the arms of two uniformed men who waited in the boat. Elizabeth balked. "Malcolm! What about Malcolm? Can you see him?" she cried.

"To the front, ladies," the older man in dress whites commanded, not giving the older woman a chance to turn back.

"I'm sure he's in one of the other boats, ma'am. We'll find him soon, I'm sure," Bree said as she guided Elizabeth to a narrow slat seat at the bow and sat beside her. A chorus of screams rang out as, with a sudden jolt, the boat started a jerky trip down to the dead calm water below. She peered up through the fog of her breath and saw a sea of faces staring down as she scanned the side of the ship. Only a few boats still hung in their davits. They'd never get them all in. She searched the railing for Malcolm's tall figure. *He was in another boat. He had to be, for Elizabeth's sake. And her own.*

73

Chapter 8

Malcolm searched high and low, but Eldon couldn't be found anywhere. A few of the men he'd spoken to remembered seeing his stepfather playing cards, but that had been hours ago. It was nearing midnight now. Malcolm chaffed, admitting to himself his mind wasn't really on the task. His thoughts were distracted by memories of the auburn-haired seamstress currently occupying his mother's suite. More than once in the past few hours he'd considered returning to spend more time with the delectable Miss Barry instead of hunting for Eldon, who clearly didn't want to be found.

He was crossing the thick carpet in the paneled library on his way to the card room as the ship seemed to lurch. It threw him off half a stride and his hip connected painfully with the corner of a heavily carved rococo table. He rubbed the bruised muscle, frowning, and continued on his way. A moment later, he stopped abruptly to avoid colliding with a frightened young man in heavy pea coat who ran by.

Within minutes he noticed crew scattering in every direction, all very much in a hurry. Just then, Malcolm spotted Robert Chisholm, whom he'd spent time with on occasion since the voyage started.

"Excuse me, Robert. Have you seen Eldon?"

Mr. Chisholm didn't seem to be aware of him. His eyes were blank and he mumbled something over and over.

Malcolm touched his shoulder. He heard the words the man kept repeating, "It can't. It can't. It just can't."

"Robert?"

The man jumped and looked at Malcolm in surprise. He shook off his daze and frowned. "What are you doing here? Get to your lifeboat station, man. There isn't much time."

It was Malcolm's turn to be perplexed. "Lifeboat? What on earth are you talking about?"

"We've struck a berg, you see. She's going down. She shouldn't. We built her to be unsinkable, you know. But she is. There's no doubt." He nearly stuttered in an effort to get the words out.

Malcolm remembered Mr. Chisholm was the chief draughtsman on the *Titanic* and, along with several White Star executives, attended the ship's maiden voyage to observe how she handled. "You're sure it will sink? When?"

"Hours. Minutes. I can't say. There's too much flooding to do a proper inspection." He stood tall and took a deep breath. "Please, Mr. DuMont. Get your life vest and report to the boat deck. If your family is still in their cabin, get them out as well." He turned and strode down the corridor toward the bridge.

Terri Benson

Malcolm reversed direction and raced toward their suite. The closer he got, the harder it became to move forward in the face of the advancing tide of bodies going the other direction. Many passengers appeared annoyed or curious, moving in groups, talking animatedly.

"Well, I never! A boat drill in the middle of the night is most uncalled for!" a portly matron grumbled, as her much-smaller husband patted her arm and urged her to keep moving.

Another strident voice carried over the din. He recognized the speaker as Mrs. Brown, a newly rich matron from Colorado. Her coarse language and commanding personality irritated Eldon to the point of madness, but Malcolm found her quite entertaining whenever they had met at dinners or other gatherings aboard the ship. She herded several reluctant passengers ahead of her, keeping up a running diatribe. "Now don't slow down, we've still got a ways to go. I don't care if it is a drill, I ain't takin' any chances. If there's nothin' to it, we'll all be snug in our beds shortly, so quit your caterwaulin' and let's get a move on." She winked at Malcolm as they passed, and he couldn't help but smile.

His smile faded as he grasped the doorknob to his mother's cabin. It was unlocked. He flung open the door. They were gone. His mother's armoire stood wide and he saw most of her clothes and coats were missing. Eldon's closet, likewise ajar, showed empty space on the floor. Malcolm sighed with relief. They must have already been warned. He fought his way one more door down the hall and entered his cabin where he donned a heavy cashmere coat with fur collar, matching scarf and a pair of thick gloves. At the last

76

moment, he sat on a bench and changed his light leather shoes for a pair of heavier boots. He strode to the door before he remembered his life vest. Another vest nestled with it, and he caught it up as well.

Back out in the corridor, the crowd grew more alarmed as rumors circulated that water covered the lower decks and there weren't enough boats for everyone. Any hope that Mr. Chisholm had been wrong was squelched by the sight of so many terrified passengers. Malcolm watched as a young man was shoved and fell. He struggled through the throng and, with savage use of his elbows and a sharp kick or two, forced the mass to move away enough so he could help the frightened boy to his feet. Wild-eyed and pale, his nose bleeding profusely, the young man clutched a bloodied hand to his chest as he looked up at Malcolm.

Malcolm realized the boy wasn't wearing a life vest and helped him into the extra one. Anxious to find his mother and Bree, he said, "Grab on to my coat and hang tight. I'm sure we'll find your family out on the deck." Keeping near the wall, they worked their way down the crowded corridor. His mind roiled with concern for his mother and the seamstress. If only he'd stayed in the cabin, he could have made sure they were safe. Instead, he'd foolishly wasted time hunting for Eldon. His musings came to an abrupt halt when he stepped out onto the deck. What he beheld took his breath away.

Chapter 9

It was bitterly cold. The lifeboat undulated over gently rolling swells a short distance from the foundering ocean liner. Bree shivered.

The crewman in the middle of the boat put the long wooden oars into the oarlocks and rowed away from the ship, each sweep accompanied by a loud creak. The senior crewman sat at the tiller and steered, his hooded eyes fixed on some unknown point on the black horizon.

As they drew farther way, more and more passengers leapt or fell into the water. Cries of distress echoed over the strangely smooth ebon water. Bree could almost smell the fear and despair surrounding her.

"Why aren't we helping? Don't you see that man over there? He's waving. Please turn back!" Bree called to the man at the stern who clutched the long wooden rudder under his arm. His eyes swiveled slowly toward her and glared, then turned away. She begged the crewman on the oars, "Please make him turn. There are people out there! Can't you hear them?"

"We ain't goin' near 'em. They'll swamp us like as not, and I ain't aimin' for a swim. Orders are to get away from the ship so she don't take us down when she goes," the older man rasped.

"But there are people out there and we have plenty of room!" Several other women echoed Bree's cry.

The man at the rudder spoke loudly. "We ain't goin' back for anyone. My orders are to stand off and wait for rescue. There are other boats. Let them go back if they want."

Bree pleaded with the other passengers. "We must help them! What if it's your husband or son out there?"

The other women murmured in agreement, calling out to the men to take them back to help.

"Shut up, I said! If you don't shut up right now you'll find yourself in the water with 'em." The tiller man's dark eyes dared the women, especially Bree, to say another word.

"I'll not sit here and let those people die, you cowards!" Bree cried, furious at their callous behavior.

The older man jerked his chin in her direction. The other crewman dropped the oars and stood, knocking women to the floor in his haste to reach the bow. Before Bree uttered another word, he picked her up and flung her into the water.

The shock was like nothing she'd ever felt--her head exploded in agony. The fur coat pulled her under like a lead weight, its bulk tangling around her legs. Bree swallowed a mouthful of briny water as she tried to kick for the boat, and gagged. The cork-and-canvas life vest tied over the coat bunched under her chin. She fumbled ineffectually at the string ties with numb fingers. Her breath was being crushed from her lungs. She splashed feebly but it was too late. The glacial water closed over her head and, as she slipped beneath the surface, her last vision was the twinkling lights of the doomed ocean liner.

Chapter 10

As far as Malcolm could see, people crammed the deck. Fights were breaking out near the few remaining lifeboats as men tried to get aboard, only to be fought back by crew. A shot rang out from farther down the ship. Women screamed and passengers dropped to the deck or ducked. Malcolm felt the boy beside him quiver with fear.

"Do you see any of your family?" he asked.

The boy stood on tiptoe and looked around. "No sir."

Malcolm led him over to a metal staircase climbing to the roof of the bridge and urged him up a few steps. "Try again."

The boy stared out over the sea of heads. He raised his arm and pointed at a nearly full lifeboat. "There! My mam and Lucy. In the boat!"

Malcolm hustled him down to the deck and shoved his way toward the lifeboat. Rough hands tried to grab him and curses rang through the air. He felt a blow to his back that almost brought him to his knees, but he caught his balance and struggled forward. They burst through the crowd and were brought up short by a row of white-clad crewmen.

"Here, now, whot'cha think you're doin'?" one asked.

"The boy--his mother and sister are on that boat." He pointed to the woman who stood and screamed, "Oliver!" Others in the boat tried to push her back to her seat as the boat swung wildly.

"Oi, Jack, help the bloke in." Another crewman stepped forward and started to hand Oliver into the boat.

Malcolm felt a surge behind him. He half turned and saw a gang of men make a rush for the boat. Not only did they outnumber the crew but they were armed with broken pieces of furniture they wielded like clubs. Quickly sizing up the situation, Malcolm waded in and downed an attacker with a strong right hook, relieving him of his club. He swung the ornate chair leg fiercely, felling aggressors indiscriminately. The crewmen followed his lead. The mob's enthusiasm faded in the face of a determined counterattack and they backed off. The bloodied crewmen closed ranks and, duty-bound, steadfastly continued to load the boat. As it lowered, a man broke from the crowd and ran to the rail. He leaped, landing on top of several women. There was a sickening *thunk* as his head struck the far side, and Malcolm knew from the angle of his neck he was dead. As soon as the boat hit the water, the two crewmen sorted him out from the frightened but uninjured women and pitched his body overboard.

With the boat gone, the crowd moved forward down the deck, searching for the next boat with room for more passengers. Malcolm stood at the now empty rail and gazed down. The smell of salt drifted in the air, mingling with oil and sweat and blood. The moon reflected off the stygian water, broken by several bobbing boats and, in the distance, glittering black mountains of ice. He frowned as he realized several vessels held far less than their capacity, and one contained only a dozen crewmen, a male passenger and a heavy-set woman. As he observed the listing deck, he saw people jump from the rails en masse, like lemmings. They tumbled on top of each other, hitting the water from great distances. He flinched at the loud splats as they struck. Most floated back to the surface face down. The few who survived attempted to swim for the boats, but either the boats moved away or the swimmers became too exhausted in the frigid water and slipped down into the black void.

He felt a presence at his shoulder and turned to see John Astor, a whirl of aromatic smoke from his cigar wreathing his head. The older man mopped his brow with a silk handkerchief, a slight tremor in his hand the only outward sign of emotion. "My God, what a mess. When you're ready, Malcolm my boy, we're in the smoking lounge. No use standing out here in the cold. We've a bottle or two and some cards." As Mr. Astor turned away, Malcolm asked, "Have you seen Eldon, sir?"

"Why, no. Not since early this evening." Mr. Astor continued on his way as if he were out for an evening stroll.

Malcolm wandered down the deck toward the stern, shaking his head at the number of people who still milled around, hoping to get into a boat. Clearly there were not enough seats. He paused next to an older crewman who stood watching, tears welling in his eyes.

"Why don't you send these people over to the boats on the other side? There isn't enough room on these for even half of them."

"The other boats are of no use. The ship is listing and we can't launch them. It doesn't matter much anyway. There aren't enough boats for everyone. Not even close."

"Not enough boats? How can that be?"

"They don't need enough boats, you see. Them's the rules. Besides, the mucky-mucks who design them don't want to spoil the pretty ship by having all those lifeboats getting in the way of the passengers. The great *Titanic* wasn't supposed to sink, you know." A tear rolled down his face. "It wasn't supposed to sink." With a sniff, he turned and shuffled slowly away from the crowd.

Malcolm staggered as the deck tilted, wending his way down the boat deck promenade toward the noticeably less occupied stern. There were no lifeboats left on the davits at this end. He almost tripped over a body tangled in the supports of the railing. It was a senior crewman. Malcolm looked closely and realized the man sported a neat bullet hole in the center of his forehead--a victim of the hysteria of the desperate passengers, no doubt.

A few people hurried down the staircase to A Deck and he saw more groups on the deck below making their way to the stern. A loose hatchway in the metal wall behind him clanged and drew Malcolm's attention to a dark corner. The dusky shadows were oddly shaped and he stepped closer. With a start, he realized the shapes were two prone bodies. Both were men, lying face up on the deck. Their heads were haloed by inky pools. He knelt next to one, realizing it was one of Eldon's card-playing cronies named Peterson. The man's eyes were open, staring, frost already coating them. The other, smaller, man was a stranger. He wore the White Star uniform. Malcolm started to stand but saw a tear slip from the crewman's eye and roll into his ear. He crawled over to the slight figure.

"I'll get help," Malcolm said, as he laid his hand on the man's chest. Though tears continued to leak from the crewman's eyes, he didn't make a sound or move a muscle, except for an almost imperceptible rise and fall of his chest. Malcolm recognized the dark halo as a puddle of blood, the unmistakable metallic odor pungent in the air. He picked up the injured man's hand. It was cold and flaccid.

Malcolm carefully reached behind the man's neck at the base of his head. He jerked his hand back when he felt a mass of soft, slimy tissue and small, hard bits. He leaned over and checked Peterson for a pulse, quickly confirming he was dead. By rolling the body over, he saw a large gash in the back of his head. The bloody gray mass and chips of bone brought a rush of bile to Malcolm's throat. Someone had violently attacked the two from behind, leaving them for dead.

He moved back to the crewman. "I'm afraid to move you by myself. I'll get help and we'll get you on a boat." The man made no reply or movement and Malcolm wondered if he were paralyzed.

He turned and raced down the listing deck toward the bow but pulled up short when he noticed there were no more lifeboats hanging from the davits. He pounded the railing in despair as he wracked his brain for a plan to get the injured man off the boat to safety.

Out of the corner of his eye, he noticed a few crewmen forging their way toward him through the mass of people crowding the railings. They turned and clattered up the staircase to the flat deck over the bridge. Malcolm watched as they pulled a large canvas off a bulge on the roof. A grinding distracted him, and several deck chairs slid across the deck to pile up at the rail, knocking passengers off their feet. The list was becoming severe. He looked up at the crewmen, realizing they must have a plan to work so diligently under the circumstances. He leaped up the steps two at a time, propelling himself with the railings. As the oiled canvas slipped aside, he stared at the deflated form for a moment before realizing it was an Englehardt collapsible lifeboat, which he'd read about in one of the innumerable articles printed about the ship before the sailing. This might be his last chance to get the injured man off the ship.

"What can I do to help?" he asked.

"Get that canvas out of the way while we pull the blocks."

As he wadded the stiff material into a bundle and pushed it off to the side he noticed there was no davit to lower the boat. "How do we get it down?"

"With ropes, unless you'd like to wait until it floats off?"

Malcolm shook his head, managing a grin at the sarcasm. He saw the nearly thirty-foot-long lifeboat would be too heavy for the three of them alone. He quickly descended and rounded up a half dozen stout men from a group who stood quietly at the back of the crowd. They appeared to have accepted their fate but, faced with a positive activity, were eager to help. The men were assigned to ropes by the lead crewman and took up their places as he directed them to lower the boat down the stair railing. Malcolm and two men were sent down below to keep the bow from slipping off the rails. It was slow work as the ship's list increased by the minute and the bow began to drop alarmingly as well. The crowd of passengers milled around on the boat deck, becoming more agitated. A few took an interest in what Malcolm and the others were doing.

"Hey, there's another boat! Them fellers found a boat! They're trying to get away with it!" Malcolm turned and saw a weasely faced man working to drum up a fight. He succeeded too, as several more men joined him and viewed the boat with covetous eyes.

"Look out!" Malcolm yelled as the mob surged forward. This time there were far more attackers and the three men at the bottom of the stairs were quickly overwhelmed. Malcolm battled fiercely, but knew they were losing ground. He sensed movement coming at him from the right, but only managed to turn a fraction before everything went dark.

Chapter 11

Bree gasped as pain seared her shoulder. Briny water trickled down her throat and her starved lungs burned. As she choked and sputtered, she felt herself pulled back to the surface. Through bleary eyes, she looked up into the face of a boy, no more than twelve or thirteen, who leaned far over the lifeboat's gunwale to grasp her wrist. Behind him, Elizabeth and two other women held on to his belt to keep him from tumbling into the water. When she was within reach, another woman grabbed her arm. The boy let go long enough to reach into his pocket and pull out a small penknife.

Her nearly frozen brain barely functioning, Bree watched dazedly as the boy cut the ties of the life vest. He tugged and it slowly drifted away. With it gone, the heavy fur coat slipped off until it hung by one arm.

"Reach up," the boy called. "Give me your other hand." He repeated the demand three times before her muddled brain managed to command her numb arm to move. As soon as he had a firm grip, the woman let go of her other hand and the waterlogged fur coat dropped like a stone into the black abyss.

Bree was dragged painfully over the gunwale by her rescuers. As her hips cleared the side, the sudden lack of resistance sent them tumbling into a heap in the bottom of the boat. Other passengers came to their assistance and in a few moments she sat shivering and nearly unconscious on her seat next to Elizabeth.

Elizabeth removed her fur coat and forced Bree's body into it, wrestling Bree around until the coat was buttoned tightly under her chin. Two women at the rear of the boat stripped off coats worn over layers of heavy clothing and passed them forward.

Elizabeth called out a grateful "Thank you!" donned one of the coats and wrapped Bree's legs with the other. Bree gasped at the sensation of a million needles stabbing her as Elizabeth roughly rubbed her hands and face. She shivered so hard she feared she would fall off the bench. Her teeth clacked together, making it impossible to talk, even if her brain had been capable of forming words. Exhausted, she clung to Elizabeth, who crooned soothingly in her ear.

Bree gradually warmed, although bouts of violent shivers still racked her body. She looked around at the other women, smiled wanly and mouthed her thanks. They nodded in return. The two crewmen watched impassively, their expressions threatening anyone else who stepped out of line with a similar punishment.

Silently they drifted farther from the groaning liner, heads nodding as they rode over the broad swells. The sounds of people thrashing in the water became faint, and soon Bree heard nothing but the gentle wash of rollers lapping the wooden hull and murmurs of the women comforting their children.

A sudden loud moan and high-pitched hiss erupted from the ship as it upended, disappearing so quickly Bree blinked in shock. Lights glowed from portholes even as they slipped under the water. Great explosions of water geysered into the air and a rumble like thunder boomed across the water. *All those people! Had they gotten off?* Bree squinted through the dark in an attempt to see how many other boats dotted the water, but it was too dark, and she couldn't see through the gauzy fog of tears freezing on her eyes.

* * * *

Bree jerked awake, shocked to have fallen asleep in such uncomfortable conditions. But many others in the boat were sleeping too, including Elizabeth, who leaned heavily against her. It seemed like hours must have passed as they floated in the bitter cold, but the night was still pitch black. A blanket of glittering stars floated across the midnight fabric above. They shimmered so brightly it brought tears to her eyes. The moon rose, a huge orange orb, sending a rippling ribbon of gold to meet them.

She stared out over the sluggish, rolling water, her mind blank until she noticed the moonlight highlighted oddly shaped flotsam in the water. Something bumped the side of the boat. She leaned over the gunwale and peered down. A retch seized her throat as she gazed into the blind, staring eyes of Mr. Thorpe. He wore a life vest over cotton striped pajamas, his skin a pale, pasty gray, rimmed with frost. She turned away, choking back sobs. When she could bring herself to look again, he was gone.

As she peered around, Bree realized among the odd shapes were many more lifeless passengers, as well as deck chairs, empty life vests and other items that must have floated off the boat as it went under. She tried to count the bodies, but at one hundred couldn't bring herself to continue.

She turned her focus back to the passengers in her lifeboat. The man at the oars sat bent over, sleeping with his arms propped on the long wooden handles, his face nearly on his knees. The rudder man sat still, one hand on the tiller, the other clutching his coat collar close about his neck. Bree thought he might be frozen stiff, but he caught her staring and glared at her with a frightening malevolence. Feeling a coward, she quickly turned away.

She didn't know how long she sat there, oblivious to her surroundings, before she heard cheers out of the dark off to the right. As Elizabeth stirred beside her, she raised her head and turned toward the sound. A large ship steamed toward them, a thick cream of water racing at the bow. The women and children murmured as one by one they saw the ship moving toward them.

Shouts of "Hurrah!" and "We're rescued!" rang out as the weary, half-frozen survivors smiled and hugged each other.

Bree, afraid to join in the cheers, wondered if she were awake, or still sleeping. Could it be true, or was she dreaming?

Chapter 12

Malcolm opened his eyes. Vague figures hovered beside him and sounds, muffled and faint, whirled around. His head pounded and he felt too tired to move. Bright lights flashed above him, leaving glittery streamers on his eyeballs after they faded. The noise around him got louder and he sorted words from the jumble.

"It's a ship. Look there, a ship!"

"Praise be to God! We're saved!"

Someone roughly patted his shoulder. "Don't you worry, feller. We'll get you safe and warm in a jiff. You should thank your lucky stars tonight, son. If you hadn't fallen damn near into the boat, we never would have caught you before you went under."

Malcolm tried to focus on the words, but they made no sense. He felt warm and wanted to take off the wet clothes weighing him down.

"Here, now. Stop it. What're you doin'? Leave that coat on, or you'll catch your death. It's the only dry piece of clothes you got. Now that we're so close to bein' rescued, it'd be a shame to kick the bucket, don't you think? Besides, it's my favorite jacket."

92

A man with kindly brown eyes leaned over and peered at him. He felt a cold hand at his nape as his head was tipped up. A draft of fiery liquid burned down his throat and Malcolm coughed and choked. As the alcohol slipped down his gullet, warmth drove off the lassitude that was trying to overtake him. In its place came uncontrollable shivers. The lights and sound faded. His world went dark again.

Chapter 13

Eldon blinked. Had he imagined a rescue ship? No, it really was there. As shivers racked his body his mind started to function again and he began to determine the best course of action. The crewmen in his lifeboat rowed frantically toward the ship and Eldon saw other boats converging on the leviathan. The rescue ship glowed with hundreds of lights and figures ran to and fro tossing ladders and nets over railings and out hull doors.

He watched as the first *Titanic* lifeboat drew up at the base of the new ship. Passengers jockeyed for position and climbed the rope ladders clattering against the side. He surveyed the other heavily laden lifeboats then the scant dozen occupants of his own. All eyes were on the rescue. It wouldn't do to be associated with the boat full of cowardly crewmen, and the even more cowardly man who disguised himself as a woman to escape the sinking ship. Before he talked himself out of it, he took a deep breath and slipped over the side.

Eldon never knew cold could hurt so badly. His throat seemed to close up as the glacial water lapped under his chin. Before he lost all feeling, he swam a few strokes to a nearby lifeboat and lunged up, grabbing the rope looped along the gunwale. He managed to croak, "Help me!" loud enough to get a passenger's attention and was quickly pulled aboard. He sat on the plank floor of the boat, his head barely above the sides, and looked across. The men in the lifeboat he'd abandoned were oblivious to his desertion.

Someone laid a coat over his shoulders and he clutched at it with blue, stiff hands. He'd taken a calculated risk, but then, that was the kind he excelled at. Eldon started to smile, but his frostbitten face refused to move.

Chapter 14

Bree huddled in the boat and watched the writhing mail sack slowly rise and swing over the railing high above. A young woman on the next seat let out a loud sigh of relief. Her two-year-old daughter had been bundled into the bag and lifted on board the rescue ship using the freight gantry. As Bree regarded the seemingly endless wall of metal next to them, she almost wished she could be hoisted aboard instead of facing the ordeal of climbing the rope net stretched down from an open door in the side of the ship. Only the vision of a seam parting and sending her back into the abyss prevented her from asking.

Two crewmen from the *Carpathia* climbed down and helped survivors get their footing. It was slow going in the frozen darkness. The women's heavy skirts tangled in the ropes and were apt to catch underfoot. A stocky, dark-skinned woman stood and began to wave her arms and jabber in an unfamiliar language. She repeatedly pointed at her feet then her waist. Her efforts were met with blank stares. She shook her head, shouldered the crewman aside, then bent over and grabbed the back hem of her skirt, pulling it through her legs and tucking it into her waistband. The remaining women watched dumbfounded as, unfettered, she clambered up the ropes like a monkey. Understanding dawned and the rest of the survivors quickly followed suit. The exodus proceeded at a much faster pace.

It was Bree's turn. She stepped aside and nodded at Elizabeth as she said to one of the rescuers, "Mrs. DuMont's hurt. I'm not sure she can climb. Isn't there some other way?"

Elizabeth tried to protest, but a look from Bree silenced her.

"Sorry, luv. This is it. Tell you what, though. I'll follow right close behind in case she needs a wee bit of help."

Bree inspected him carefully, as if he were a horse she considered buying. He was big, over six feet. Bulging biceps and shoulders stretched his coat tight. He had a fresh, kind face and his fair cheeks showed the light strawberry blonde fur of an unshaven youth. Bree smiled and nodded. Elizabeth would be in good hands.

Only Bree, the two *Titanic* crewmen and the other man from the rescue ship remained in the lifeboat. She nodded at the man slumped and unmoving at the oars. "What about him?"

The *Carpathia* crewman nudged her toward the now-empty ladder. "It's too late for him, miss. Now get your skirt fixed and let's be gettin' on the ship. It's awful cold down here and there's warm blankets and coffee up there."

She nodded her thanks and turned, giving a last look at the remaining *Titanic* crewman. He studiously avoided her gaze. How would he fare once his actions were known? Even after what had happened, she found herself pitying the man. With a mental shrug, she hooked her foot into the net and took the first step.

* * * *

Malcolm struggled out of the dark and forced his crusted eyes open. There was an incessant roar in his ears and his head pounded mercilessly. He lay still, blinking, as he tried to sort out what was going on. The roar resolved into hundreds of voices laughing, crying, praying and shouting. He gingerly turned his head and looked out over a sea of humanity. Sitting, standing, lying--they littered every square inch of a large enclosed space.

He surveyed his body. He was swathed in a heavy blanket, bare shoulders sticking out at one end, equally bare feet at the other. He lay on a raised bench or table pushed up to a wall. As Malcolm tried to sit up, the stabbing pain in the back of his head and neck brought on a bout of nausea and he slumped back, eyes closed.

A man with a gravelly voice spoke from nearby. "Still with us, are you, my boy?"

Malcolm opened his eyes again and saw a lined face, vaguely familiar. "Yes, sir," he managed to croak.

"Wait a moment. I'll fetch you a drink." The man picked his way through the crush of people to tables at the far side of the room. Pots of all sizes and shapes were laid out, some steaming, with bowls and cups grouped around them. Malcolm battled to focus his eyes as the man ladled water into one mug, a dark brew into another.

He returned and held out a mug. "Can you sit up to drink some water, or do you need help?"

Malcolm carefully rolled to the side, pausing as the room spun. He took a deep breath and pushed up with his elbow, sliding sideways until he propped against the wall. He reached out a shaky hand and took the mug. The lukewarm water was like nectar as it slid down his parched throat. He got two big gulps before the mug ran dry. The man replaced it with another chipped cup filled with steamy broth. Malcolm closed his eyes and inhaled the heavenly aroma before sipping. He sighed and sagged against the wall.

He gazed intently at his benefactor. "I'm sorry, sir. I'm sure I know you, but I can't quite recall your name."

"John Thayer. You know my son, Jack."

Through the cotton wool that filled his mind, Malcolm recalled the face of a young, athletic man with whom he'd recently played squash. He smiled and nodded, scanning the crowd. "Where is Jack?"

The lines in the man's face deepened and it seemed he aged at least a decade as he said, "I can't find him, or his mother. There are so many people." He swayed and Malcolm reached out a hand to steady him. "They've put us all over the ship, wherever there's room. I'm told I'll have to wait until we get to New York before they'll have a complete list of survivors. I'm afraid they're... I'm so afraid." Tears slipped down Mr. Thayer's face. The hand that scrubbed across his lined forehead trembled. Then he seemed to collect himself and stood a little taller. "They let me wander around, though. In case I see them." He absently patted Malcolm on the shoulder and turned away.

"I'm sure they're here somewhere, sir. I'll help you search for him. I need to locate my mother too." Malcolm looked down and frowned. "I just need to find some clothes first." Mr. Thayer stumbled away as if he hadn't heard.

It took Malcolm nearly an hour to obtain a pair of dirty trousers and a mismatched suit jacket a few sizes too wide, with sleeves that stopped halfway to his wrists. The damp jacket smelled of saltwater and oil. His head still hurt like the dickens, but he was able to stand and walk without the floor and walls undulating around him. At the food table, he picked up a thin slice of cheese and a piece of bread and butter, and gulped down a mug of strong, hot coffee. Fortified, Malcolm made his way purposefully around the room, checking each knot of people for his mother or Jack. Unsuccessful, he spoke to a few *Carpathia* crewmen, and they sent him off to other areas of the ship where *Titanic* passengers were being housed.

* * * *

Eldon perched on the edge of an unmade bed in the rescue ship's crew quarters, alone. It had cost him his gold pocket watch, but it was worth it to get away from the bedlam of whining children and their sniveling mothers. He spent a few moments wondering what had become of Elizabeth and Malcolm, thinking it unlikely he'd have to face his incensed stepson any time soon. Elizabeth was inconsequential and would be easy to deal with. His brother's son, however, had frequently proven rather irascible. It would be simpler if Malcolm had gone down with the ship, but it would probably be a few days before he knew for sure. He stretched out on the lumpy mattress, arms behind his head, and formulated a series of plans.

Chapter 15

The cough started almost as soon as Bree set foot on the *Carpathia*'s deck. It came in unexpected waves, erupting out of her chest in rolling surges of pain. Elizabeth became alarmed when Bree couldn't catch her breath and went to fetch a man who was treating other passengers. Dr. O'Loughlin turned out to be a *Titanic* passenger who'd also been rescued. He placed his ear on her chest and tried to listen, but she broke out in another fit of coughing. He helped Bree into a seated position and folded her pillow in half, adding a blanket from nearby to the bundle, then laid her back so she half-reclined.

He shook his head, frowning. "Were you in the water, young lady?"

Elizabeth answered for her. "Yes. One of the men in our lifeboat threw her into the water and she nearly drowned."

He gave the older woman an incredulous look. "Threw her over? Why ever would he do that?"

"Bree wanted them to go back to help people in the water. She called them cowards. It's the rest of us that were cowards, though.

We sat there and let them do it. It's just we never expected--"

The doctor laid a calming hand on her shoulders. "Of course not. None of us expected any of this. The men will surely be punished for their actions before this is all over. But right now, I'm concerned about your young friend here. It's too early to be sure, but if she got water in her lungs, she'll likely end up with pneumonia. It'll be a few days before we can get her to a hospital. I don't suppose she's going to be very comfortable in the meantime, but we'll have to do the best we can."

He started to turn away. Bree caught at his sleeve. "Elizabeth has some broken ribs, sir. Please don't let her do anything she ought not to." Bree wheezed. The effort of talking exhausted her and caused another fit of coughing.

Dr. O'Loughlin turned and shook his finger at Elizabeth, a threatening mock frown on his face. "You heard the young lady." His attempt to reassure her fell on deaf ears as she continued to wring her hands. He patted her shoulder and smiled encouragingly. "Stay close to her. Both of you get some rest. I'll check back now and again. Try to get her to eat a bit and drink as much as possible." He walked off a few paces before being summoned by a group crouched over a supine body.

Elizabeth fetched cups and a small pitcher of water then lay down beside Bree.

Even with the coughing, Bree caught a few brief naps. Each time she woke to Elizabeth's worried regard. "Elizabeth, you must sleep. You'll be sick too, if you're not careful."

"I've dropped off a few times, dear. I'm not used to so much noise. It's hard to sleep, but I imagine I'll get used to it soon."

They huddled together and watched the disparate assemblage of passengers spread out around the hold as the rescue ship plowed on toward New York.

* * * *

Malcolm was desperate. He'd been all over the ship and had yet to find his mother. Whenever he saw anyone he knew, he asked if they'd seen her. Many of the women were in a daze, hardly acknowledging his questions, their children nestled tightly in their arms. A few managed to answer, but always with a "No, sorry." He stopped more frequently to let the headache and dizziness pass before he continued. Fuzzy shadows haloed everything and he began to run into corners and tables as his depth perception faded. He'd been searching for hours and was nearly at the end of his rope when a flash of color caught his eye. An auburn mass at the edge of his vision stirred a memory and he turned sharply, stumbling. He gazed across the room. It swayed crazily. His vision narrowed to a long dark tunnel. The tiny light at the end went out.

Chapter16

As she lay in the stark white room, Bree tried to put her jumbled thoughts in order. Disjointed pictures flashed in her head--vaguely remembered soothing words and cold cloths on her forehead. Feeling like she was being roasted alive. A handsome chestnut-haired man with a devastating smile. A pair of dark, leering eyes made her sick to her stomach. Dark blue eyes soothed her fear. Emeralds and diamonds shone under gaslight. A young boy desperately reached out to her.

Bree recalled the terror of black water closing over her head as she clutched the thin blanket under her chin. One moment she was shivering, the next burning.

The door opened and a woman in a starched white uniform marched into the room and took Bree's temperature. The nurse silently fluffed the pillows, tucked the blanket in and tidied the room, all the while never looking at Bree or offering a word of comfort.

A few minutes later, the door opened again and a tall, stately man entered and smiled as he walked to the bedside. At his appearance, the nurse brightened and stepped close to the other side of the bed.

"Good afternoon, young lady," he said to Bree. "It's good to see you awake. How do you feel?"

Bree licked her parched lips.

"Nurse Danville?" At his nod, the nurse grasped a handle and cranked until the head of the bed rose to a semi-reclined position. She held a cup for Bree to drink a few sips of tepid water then stood beside the bed and gazed longingly at the doctor.

"To be honest, I don't feel too well. What happened?" Bree asked.

"You've had a raging case of pneumonia. Other than that and a good dunking in the North Atlantic, not much." He gave her a sympathetic smile showing lots of brilliant white teeth, and Nurse Danville sloshed water onto Bree's head.

The doctor frowned at the nurse as she apologized and stepped back, setting the cup down with a shrug of her shoulders and a silly grin.

Memories of the great *Titanic* tipping up and sliding down to her death flooded Bree's mind. "Mrs. DuMont!" She tried to sit up.

"Settle down young lady." He pressed her shoulders down. "I've about got you healthy. Don't go and spoil it."

"What about Elizabeth? Elizabeth DuMont. She was with me on the ship. And when we were rescued." An overwhelming sense of panic welled up inside her at the thought she'd been abandoned.

"Well, if you mean that very handsome older woman who has been camped outside your room for the last week, Mary can fetch her

105

right in. She's doing fine. I finally persuaded her to let me check her ribs, and she's much better now."

Nurse Danville's head had snapped around as she heard the doctor's description of Elizabeth. Her lips compressed as she stalked across the room, opened the door to briefly beckon then hustled back to the doctor's side. Elizabeth's blonde head peeked around the door and the doctor motioned her in.

As she hurried up to the bed and saw Bree's relieved smile, she heaved a mighty sigh and bent to fold her into a tight embrace. "Oh, I've been so worried about you," she whispered into Bree's ear. She straightened and wiped tears from her face with a crumpled handkerchief. "Thank you so much, Doctor Tumey. You're a godsend." She laid her hand upon his arm. Bree was sure the good doctor blushed.

Nurse Danville, who watched the exchange closely, a frown denting her forehead, insinuated herself between Elizabeth and Doctor Tumey and made a production of taking Bree's blood pressure. Elizabeth didn't seem to notice, but Bree caught the grimace of annoyance the doctor directed at the nurse. With a disappointed look at Elizabeth's back, Doctor Tumey shrugged slightly and said, "I'd best be off to see my other patients, as this one is in such lovely...er...good hands." He blushed again and quickly bowed out of the room.

As soon as he disappeared from sight, Nurse Danville turned on her heel and left, slamming the door on her way out.

"How long have I been here, Mrs. DuMont?" Bree asked. "Doctor

Tumey said something about a week?"

"You've been here six days, dear. And I think by now it would be much simpler, and I would like it very much, if you called me Elizabeth." She sat on the bed close to Bree's hip.

Bree smiled. "I'd like that."

Elizabeth's expression turned businesslike. "Now, since you're on the mend, we must make some plans. I'd like to take you back home with us, so we can all rest up." She paused, a look of chagrin on her face. "Oh, dear. It hadn't occurred to me until just now you might have friends or family searching for you. It's been such a muddle. With Malcolm hurt and you sick, and, well, I haven't much energy myself. Eldon has been off taking care of business and I've been trying to deal with the shipping line." Elizabeth slumped and shook her head. "I'm such a foolish old woman. I can't manage to do the simplest things, and here you might have family frantic about you."

Bree reached out with both hands and clasped Elizabeth's. "Please don't worry. I have no family or friends here. Except you," she added, pleased to see the older woman's face brighten. Then, trying to sound nonchalant, Bree asked, "Now, what was that you said about Malcolm being injured?"

"He's doing much better now. He's been up and about for the last few days, but the doctor didn't want him to leave just yet. He was hit on the head and fell into the water."

Bree gasped.

"Oh, don't worry. He always did have a hard head," Elizabeth said with a wave of her hand and a roll of her eyes. Her face turned serious. "He had a concussion and made it a bit worse by running all over the *Carpathia* trying to find us." At Bree's confused expression, she explained, "That's the name of the ship which rescued us. It brought us to New York. There was so much confusion. I don't know if they've sorted out all the people who were rescued or even know who died. There were so very many." She closed her eyes, shaking her head.

"And Eldon? It sounds like he survived." Bree didn't even attempt to stifle the dislike in her voice.

Elizabeth didn't appear to notice her tone. "Oh, yes. Apparently, he jumped in the water to rescue people and barely managed to grab on to a lifeboat before he drowned. That's Eldon for you. Came out without a scratch, and a hero to boot. Picture in the paper and everything. He has invitations to breakfast, lunch and dinner every day from people who want to thank him."

"Do you go with him?" Bree knew what the answer would be before Elizabeth spoke.

"No. No, I've been so worried about you and Malcolm. My ribs have been hurting quite a bit, too. It seemed easier to stay here. Dr. Tumey arranged rooms for us at the Brevoort Hotel not far away. It's a lovely place. The doctor's been very kind."

Bree noticed a slight flush on Elizabeth's face as she talked about the doctor, and smiled.

"Now, back to the question at hand. Will you come to Massachusetts with us? We have such a big house. It's absolutely beautiful this time of year. We can enjoy a nice visit while you get your health back. Then you can decide what you would like to do next." Elizabeth said, nodding as if the decision were already made.

Bree frowned and chewed her lip. She didn't want to be alone-- not with everything in such an uproar. She certainly didn't want to abandon her new friend to Eldon's not-so-tender mercies. And, of course, there was Malcolm. This sounded like an awfully good idea. Then an awfully bad thought popped into her head. "Oh, no. My money. Everything!" she wailed.

Chapter 17

Eldon enjoyed his newfound celebrity status. He hadn't spent a dime since the ship had docked. Every time he turned around someone wanted to buy him a drink or a meal, or whatever else took his fancy.

He took the steps into St. Vincent's hospital two at a time. If he were lucky, Malcolm would have taken a turn for the worse and Elizabeth would be too busy to interrupt his plans for the evening. He stopped short as he came around a corner and saw a large group of people milling in the hallway. Irritated, he snapped, "See here, what's all this about? I need to get through." He shoved against the throng until he heard his wife's shrill voice call out.

"Eldon, dear. How wonderful. You're just in time to attend the ceremony." Elizabeth hurried forward, her arm linked in that of a tall, dark-haired woman. "Louise, this is my husband, Eldon. Eldon, this is Louise Vanderbilt." The woman inclined her head regally.

And so she should. Vanderbilt! The family controlled a vast fortune spanning the entire country. "How do you do?" He bent over

110

her hand with a gallant flourish.

"Quite well, thank you." She turned, dismissing him. "Now, Elizabeth, shall we continue? I would hate to delay the young woman's voyage into matrimony, being as her voyage to America has been such a tragedy."

Eldon stepped up beside his wife, eyebrow raised, not about to miss out on one second in the company of a Vanderbilt.

Elizabeth explained, "It's so romantic. This young lady, Sarah Roth, came to America to wed her betrothed. She lost everything on the ship, even the wedding dress she made. Louise and the Women's Relief Committee have provided her with a lovely trousseau and they're being wed right here at the hospital."

Eldon searched his mind for an excuse to avoid the maudlin event without offending Miss Vanderbilt.

Malcolm appeared at his mother's side and in a derisive tone said, "Ah, Eldon, you've decided to grace us with your heroic presence?"

Damn the boy! Eldon wished he could do something to wipe the false smile off his stepson's face, but that simply wouldn't do. Instead, he plastered on a phony smile of his own and nodded. "I wouldn't miss such a joyous occasion for anything, dear boy." He took Elizabeth's arm and escorted her down the hall to the chapel. He deftly worked his way next to Miss Vanderbilt and made sure to voice the proper exclamations of excitement and happiness, while he smiled and nodded like a fool. His reward came when Louise invited the four of them to dinner at her mansion that evening.

"How kind, Louise," Elizabeth said, "but I can't leave poor Bree here alone."

Apparently, Elizabeth and Louise had discussed the seamstress earlier, as Louise nodded. "Of course. I understand. Perhaps another time." Eldon bit his tongue to keep from screaming at his wife. This was his big opportunity, his chance to rub elbows with the highest echelon of power in the country. He would finally have a venue to show the right people just how clever he was. It would be perfect.

Malcolm, of all people, came to his rescue. "You do go on, Mother. I'll sit with Bree tonight. You deserve some fun after caring for the two of us so well. And all by yourself."

Eldon flushed with anger at the jab and forced a benign smile. "That's right, dear. I've been trying to drag you away from this place for days. You're beginning to look quite haggard again. And you were really beginning to make such good progress getting your strength back."

Elizabeth put her hand to her cheek, as if making sure her face hadn't lost more of its appeal.

Louise patted her shoulder. "It's settled then. Why not come with me right now in the car? It will save you trying to get a taxi. The streets are still packed with people coming and going to the pier and family and friends arriving for visits. We'll have time to chat before dinner. I'd like to talk with you about a few of my pet projects."

Eldon cringed. Pet projects to the Vanderbilts ran into the millions. If Louise got her hooks into Elizabeth, she would likely give her--*his*--entire fortune to the filthy masses. He turned up the amperage on his false smile and nodded agreeably as he steered the women toward the entrance. He shot a quick glance over his shoulder and saw Malcolm's decidedly unfriendly glare. Eldon turned around and smirked to himself. *There's not a thing he can do to me.* He schemed to insinuate himself into the Vanderbilt's business while he pretended attention to the women's prattling.

Chapter 18

Bree sat in bed, hands knotted in her lap. Elizabeth had eventually taken her leave after trying to reassure Bree the loss of all her money and personal belongings wasn't the end of the world. They'd argued when Elizabeth offered to replace everything, but Bree hadn't had the strength to continue. As a compromise, Elizabeth accepted Bree's offer to go through the older woman's clothing and make alterations as needed to repay any costs incurred. It was a hard sell. Bree was sure Elizabeth only agreed so she would calm down--that, and the fact an important wedding was due to take place at the hospital in a few moments.

Alone for the time being, Bree took the opportunity to wash her hair. She welcomed the short respite from her narrow bed, although bathing in the tiny hospital tub was a chore. Despite her misgivings, she was excited about going north with the DuMonts. Elizabeth's glowing description of the heavily wooded rolling hills, tumbling brooks, white clapboard buildings and deep grass pastures sounded wonderful. Any view would be an improvement on the dirty brick wall a few feet outside her grimy window. She'd been in America for more than a week, and all she'd seen were those bricks.

She sat in a chair by the flyspecked window and brushed her hair dry. She was bored and restless. Dr. Tumey had regretfully denied her request to go to the wedding, concerned her weakened condition would too easily allow her to catch something else.

"Oh, well, Elizabeth will return soon. She promised to tell me all about the ceremony," she muttered as she stood and wandered around, eventually plopping down on the hard, hated mattress. Bree released some of her pent-up frustration by giving her pillow a good beating and settled back on the plumped feathers when a series of knocks sounded on the door.

It wasn't Elizabeth who entered at her invitation; Malcolm stood grinning in the doorway. "May I come in?"

"Of course." Bree craned her neck to peer around him. "Isn't your mother with you?"

"Sorry, no. You're going to have to make do with me this evening. Mother and Eldon have another engagement. I'm here to keep you company."

Bree sank back against the pillow. She was desperately lonely, but wasn't sure she was up to the torture of having Malcolm near. "There's no need. I'm quite capable of being by myself. I'll talk with your mother about the wedding tomorrow."

He shook his head. "Ah, but you needn't wait. I can describe it to you. It was quite lovely. The bride wore a white gown, of course, in the popular Empire style. Seed pearls lavishly embellished the bodice and sleeves, as well as her tiny pillbox hat."

Bree giggled at his theatrical recitation. He flapped his arms and his expressive eyebrows waggled up and down as he paced the room, turning dramatically as he mimicked the bride sweeping down the aisle. He went on to describe the diverse group of people in attendance, changing his voice and parroting their actions. Bree laughed until her side ached and tears rolled down her face.

"Stop, please. I can't take any more of this." She held up her hands in appeal.

"All right. But Mother's version won't be nearly so much fun. She's much too nice to tell you all the silly parts." He stopped near the bed and gazed down at her. "Aren't you about sick of lying in that bed?"

"I can't begin to tell you how much I wish I could get up."

"Then why don't you?" he asked.

"Where would I go? I haven't any clothes, and Dr. Tumey would have a fit if I got sick again."

"Stay right there. I have a plan." With a conspiratorial wink and broad grin, he slipped out of the room, leaving her with her mouth hanging open.

"And where would I go, pray tell?" she grumbled in annoyance, but her interest was piqued.

A few moments later Malcolm returned, pushing a wicker wheelchair. A blanket lay folded over the seat. "Ta da! Your chariot awaits, my sweet."

The endearment brought a blush to her cheeks, and she quickly looked down at her lap, hoping her unbound hair would hide her face.

"Well, what are you waiting for? You said you wanted out of bed. Get a move on."

His enthusiasm was contagious, and brought a smile to her face. Glad she wore a clean flannel nightgown that covered her adequately from chin to toes and nearly to her fingertips, she rolled out of bed and took a step toward the chair. She stopped and grasped the iron footboard as a wave of dizziness flooded over her. He reached out and caught her elbow, helping to steady her.

"I know the feeling. I've finally gotten over being dizzy all the time." He waited patiently as she took a moment to get her equilibrium back.

Smiling her thanks, she managed to take the last few steps, her toes curling against the cold floor tiles. He whisked the blanket off the seat, shook it out and laid it over the whole chair. He took her hand and bowed as he settled her on her throne. Once seated, he carefully tucked the blanket around her shoulders and folded it so the only parts of her showing were her head and hands.

"And for my next trick." He pulled white objects out of his coat pocket with a flourish. He bent down, pulled first one bare foot then the other out from under the blanket, and slid on thick cotton socks. "Wouldn't want Dr. Tumey after me for letting you catch a chill." He grinned again and her dizziness returned, but it had very little to do with getting out of bed too fast, and a lot to do with his unexpected thoughtfulness.

He pushed her out of the room and down the hall. Almost

immediately, an attractive woman at a long counter called out a greeting. Malcolm responded in a friendly and polite manner and moved on. Bree saw disappointment in the woman's expression. After several similar exchanges, Bree experienced an unfamiliar emotion. *Surely she wasn't jealous?* "Do you know everyone here?" she finally asked.

He leaned his head down close to her ear. His breath tickled as he laughed. "Not everyone, but I've been cooped up here as long as you. The difference is they let me move around. In fact, they kept getting after me not to fall asleep. I took to walking the halls to stay awake. I've met most of the people who work in this wing, and have gotten to know the families of other *Titanic* survivors who were brought here." He straightened up and turned down another hall.

Bree wanted him to lean back down. His essence was clean and manly, a rich blend of musk and spice. Definitely *not* the antiseptic odor permeating her room. She decided to keep him talking. "There are a lot of women who work here." She glanced over her shoulder and found his eyes on her. "They seem to like you."

She bit her lip as he grinned. "Don't act so surprised. I'm a very likeable fellow. What can I say?"

"Are there a lot of *Titanic* passengers here?

"More than one hundred to begin with. Almost everyone has left, but there are a few stragglers, like you and me." He bent down again and she caught her breath. "I've heard," he whispered, sending chills down her back, "they're going to run us out of here tomorrow."

She turned quickly in excitement, and her lips met his. Shocked by the soft warmth, she stared into his amused blue eyes. He made no attempt to move, and she knew she'd waited a few seconds longer than propriety allowed before turning away. A massive wave of heat rolled up her neck, clear to her forehead. She squeezed her eyes shut in mortification, expecting Malcolm to say something that would embarrass her even more.

Instead, he said, "We're here."

They turned into a large cafeteria dotted with tables and chairs. Bree wasn't sure if she was more upset about the inadvertent kiss, or the fact he didn't even seem to notice.

He noted her silence. "Are you all right?" He stopped the chair and stepped in front of her. "You're a little flushed. It's not a fever is it?" He laid his large hand on her forehead, like her mother used to do. "You don't feel hot." The corners of his mouth quirked up. "If you're not sick, what else could it be?"

Bree glared at him. Obviously, he *had* noticed their kiss and knew exactly what caused her rosy cheeks. Before she could think of a suitable retort, he slipped behind and wheeled her over to a table. Malcolm sat in the nearest chair and drew her attention to a printed menu on the table. "What would you like for dinner? I can't promise you gourmet, but it will probably be better than what you've gotten in those horrid trays they deliver."

Still trying to figure out if he deliberately teased her, or wasn't affected in any way by the unexpected kiss, Bree tried to concentrate on the printed words. "I'd about give my arm for a nice pot roast," she said.

"I don't believe the prices are quite that steep. One post roast coming up, my lady." He bowed again and headed for the counter where he spoke to a plump woman in a tall white hat. She smiled at Bree and nodded. Malcolm returned and sat. He seemed intent on disarming her, keeping up a running monologue on the different passengers and their families he'd met, what their injuries were, where they were from, and other bits of their lives.

Even after plates heaped with food were set in front of them, he kept talking, stopping only to urge her to eat. And eat she did.

"You really were hungry for a decent meal, weren't you?" He observed her nearly spotless plate.

Bree bit her lip. What would he think of her? She'd shoveled her food down nearly as fast as her brothers had. She quickly looked down at her bosom, praying she wasn't as sloppy as them when eating. With relief, she saw only her pristine nightgown.

"I'm glad to see you have an appetite. I hate skinny women. In France, it seems all the models they use for the fashion shows are near death from lack of food. Besides, I'd wager to say you've lost more than a pound or two in the last week."

Again, Bree felt off center, unsure. She gazed into his eyes, the color of the deep Atlantic at midday. "I'm sorry. I wasn't paying any attention to the food, I mean, while you were talking, I just..." She groaned. It seemed she couldn't say anything right.

Malcolm reached out and patted her hand.

If he does one more thing to treat me like a child, I will scream! Bree pulled her fingers from under his and clasped her hands in her lap. She attempted to get herself under control by taking a deep breath. "What were your mother and Eldon doing tonight?"

"Louise Vanderbilt invited them to dinner. Mother was going to refuse, but for once, I agreed with Eldon. She needed a night away from here. She's been flitting between your room and mine since we got here. If Dr. Tumey hadn't made her stop and eat now and then, she'd probably be a patient as well." Malcolm sat back in his chair, a frown creasing his forehead above the bridge of his nose.

"Dr. Tumey seems very competent."

"He's actually quite well known. We were lucky to be brought here, especially when he was on duty. I think," he leaned in toward her, one expressive eyebrow raised, "he might be sweet on Mother."

Bree smiled. "I thought so too. Of course, she did absolutely nothing to encourage him," she added, not wanting him to get the wrong idea.

"Hmm. I wish she would. At least he might acknowledge her devotion, unlike Eldon. Although he's been a bit more attentive since the sinking. The bas-- Urm, my stepfather, apologized profusely to Mother. He claimed he drank too much, lost a large sum of money at cards, and had a grave lapse of judgment. And he gave her a magnificent set of jewelry to replace some of what she lost. As if that would make up for what he did," Malcolm gritted out. Sadness crept over his face. "I don't think she believed it, but after he left she told me in no uncertain terms never to bring it up again." He brightened a little as he added, "But there's something a bit different about her. She doesn't look to him every time she makes a decision now. Maybe it's a start."

"I hope so. She's such a wonderful woman. She doesn't deserve to be treated that way." Bree said.

He gave her a grateful smile and nodded. "Now you've had dinner, how about a trip around the block?"

"I'm not sure. I mean, I can't go outside in my nightclothes."

"Maybe not, but we can at least take a tour around the inside of the building. There are miles of hallway here." He pushed her out of the dining room and they spent a couple peaceful hours while he gave her a guided tour of the different floors. They found an unattended elevator and rode it up and down after Malcolm took to closing his eyes and pushing a button, taking her out on whatever floor they ended up on. That came to a halt when they mistakenly stepped out onto the surgical floor and were chased off by an irate nurse.

Bree felt exhausted by the time he wheeled her back to her room. She climbed out of the chair and slipped under the bedclothes. He must have noticed her tired eyes because he said, "I shouldn't have kept you out so late, Miss Barry. It won't be Dr. Tumey I have to worry about if Mother finds out I caused you to relapse."

She smiled. "It was lovely, Mr. Du...um...Malcolm. I enjoyed getting out. I can't believe how big this place is, and you know so much about it. You don't seem sick. I would have expected they'd let you go sooner than this."

He smiled. "I'm glad you've finally decided to call me by my given name. And since we're going to be spending so much time in each other's company in the coming weeks, will you finally consider me a friend?" He watched her intently, and she could have sworn he held his breath.

She smiled sheepishly. "I suppose. And as I said before, my friends call me Bree."

He let out his breath in a whoosh. "Excellent! You need to get some sleep now. It's late and you're probably tuckered out. I'm going to park your chariot here in the corner. If they don't let us leave tomorrow, I'll come in and steal you away." He smiled charmingly and went out, closing the door gently behind him.

Bree stared at the door. *I'm afraid he's already stolen my heart, and doesn't even know it.*

Chapter 19

Malcolm meandered through the halls late into the night. He couldn't get those emerald eyes out of his head. The memory of her soft lips brushing his caused an uncomfortable pressure in his loins. Knowing she was there, only a thin layer of flannel separating them as they sat at the table, had been torture. He hoped her disconcerted attitude stemmed from the same source as his own--being so close to her, talking to her about anything that popped into his head, hearing her laugh at his silly attempts at amusement. It had been a wonderful evening. For him at least.

She was the reason he was still here at the hospital. Dr. Tumey suggested he was fit enough to leave a few days ago, so he'd started feigning dizzy spells. He wanted to be near Bree, to make sure she got the care she needed. It was agony knowing he couldn't do anything to help her himself. When his mother told him she had convinced Bree to go home with them, he only just refrained from giving her a crushing hug. If her ribs were healed, he would have anyway. It was the perfect solution. It would buy him time to convince Bree he wasn't the rich ne'er-do-well she obviously thought him to be. No way would he watch her walk out of his life now. Eldon made a fuss, demanding to know why his wife would want to drag along a half-downed seamstress. Malcolm smiled at the vision of his mother drawing herself up to her full height and lecturing her overbearing husband.

"Not only do I owe her my life, but I consider her a very dear friend. She could have easily left me sleeping in my room. She might have taken every piece of jewelry I owned, and anything else she wanted. But she didn't. She took care of me. And I'll not do anything less for her. She has no family. No one to care for, or about, her. I intend to do both."

She'd glared at Eldon with a fire Malcolm hadn't seen in her eyes for years. He hoped it was a sign she wasn't going to let her husband dominate her life anymore. Time would tell.

He finally made his way back to his room in the wee hours of the morning. Still plenty of time to dream about creamy white skin and imagine long, coppery curls twisting around his body and drawing him close.

* * * *

His mother breezed in with his breakfast the next morning. "Dr. Tumey says you are well enough to leave."

"What about Miss Barry?" He tried to appear unconcerned.

Elizabeth eyed him slyly. "What about Miss Barry, dear?" When she saw the exasperated look he gave her, she relented, grinning. "Bree too. I asked Eldon to make arrangements for our private rail car to be brought up. I think we'd be much more comfortable than riding in a motorcar all that way. Now you sit still and eat your breakfast while I go tell Bree."

As his mother left the room, Malcolm smiled. He would have at least a few days where Bree couldn't get away from him. Perhaps enough time to convince her she should spend the rest of her life with him. When he'd left for Europe with his mother and Eldon, he thought all he wanted was to take over the family business and make it what his father had wanted, not what Eldon changed it into. But now, the only thing on his mind was a beautiful, Titian-haired young woman named Bridget Barry.

* * * *

Bree was thrilled to hear she would no longer be confined to bed in the tiny room. She wasn't sure how often Malcolm would take time to visit an invalid, and now at least he wouldn't have to see her surrounded by the sights and smells of a hospital. Soon they'd be on their way to the fresh air of the country. She was truly about to begin her adventure in America.

As Dr. Tumey left her room after giving her a clean bill of health, and a warning to take it easy for a few more weeks, Elizabeth entered. She ignored his flustered smile, and the despairing grimace that followed, as she carried several boxes over to the bed. A grinning Malcolm hustled along behind, more packages heaped in his arms. Bree stood by the window in a rumpled flannel gown and robe and turned as Elizabeth laughingly tumbled the boxes onto her bed, her son following suit.

"What's all this?" Bree asked as she ambled over.

"Open them and see, my dear." Elizabeth stepped behind her and hugged Bree's shoulders, her chin resting next to her ear. "You can't very well leave here in a nightdress, now can you? We picked up a few things for you until we get home. Then we can get you a proper wardrobe."

Bree bent her head, gazing at her stocking-clad feet. "Elizabeth, you've been so kind. I promise I'll pay back every cent."

"I beg your pardon!"

Bree's head snapped up at the tone of outrage in Elizabeth's voice. She turned, wide eyed and beheld her friend's angry face.

"If you think I do this expecting to be repaid, you are sadly mistaken, young lady. I enjoyed every minute of shopping for you." Her gray eyes softened. "I never had the chance to spoil a daughter. Shopping for you was such fun." She smiled at Bree and held her arms out. "Please let me do this. No strings attached. Please."

Bree didn't hesitate, leaning into Elizabeth's embrace. Elizabeth whispered into her ear, "Buying clothes for you is eminently more enjoyable than buying them for Malcolm. Black and gray suits are so *boring*."

Bree stepped back, laughing. "I thank you very much for your generosity." Then she picked up a box. "Now, what should I wear?"

* * * *

Malcolm wandered over to the window and leaned on the frame. He watched, enjoying the lighthearted banter between the two so-different women. Elizabeth helped Bree select an outfit, then shooed him from the room. He paced the hallways, never out of sight of the door, and was only a step away when it opened and Bree came out. She looked like the well-bred woman he'd first met on the ship, clothed in a dusky green suit that set her hair off to perfection. It fit well, but not quite as well as the gray outfit had. Her hair was pulled back from her face with green jade combs and her tiny feet were shod in fashionable pointy-toed lace-up boots.

"Excuse me, miss, have you seen a half-drowned girl? I left her in this room, but now she's gone."

Bree chuckled. "I'll take that as a compliment, whether you meant it or not."

He bowed and followed her back into the room. Elizabeth sorted packages into an orderly stack. She linked elbows with Bree and gave him an inquiring stare.

"Well, since I've been relegated to pack horse, I suggest we be on our way." He enjoyed bringing up the rear of the procession. It gave him the opportunity to watch Bree's gently swaying hips. The swishing fabric had a mesmerizing effect and he nearly tripped over the top step as they exited the building. A big seven-passenger Oldsmobile touring car waited outside. With only the three of them and minimal luggage, the car felt immense. The driver, clad in a black suit with cap pulled low over his brow, stowed their bags in the boot and helped Elizabeth into the middle seat. Malcolm opened the other door for Bree, and watched as she settled into the thickly tufted leather bench beside his mother. He climbed into the front seat next to the chauffeur. Before the driver merged into traffic, Malcolm asked him to take a short detour to the pier.

As they pulled up along the waterfront, redolent with the scents of day-old fish and diesel oil, he pointed. "The *Carpathia*. If not for her, none of us would be here." The three of them stared up at the cargo ship, which sported four huge derricks and a single large stack, for several moments, each deep in their own thoughts. Bree looked at Elizabeth. Her face was drawn and pale. They clasped hands and shared a moment of silence.

The driver cleared his throat loudly. "If we don't get a move on you'll miss your train, folks."

Malcolm nodded and they turned away from the pier. Traffic was heavy and it took nearly a half hour to get back to Greenwich Village and Penn Station. It was time to go home.

* * * *

Eldon sat in a corner trying to ignore the unwashed masses bustling around the huge terminal. He hated traveling by train. There were too many working class rubes who didn't have the sense to know their place. It was one more reason he simmered with anger at Elizabeth. He'd been forced to delay his return to the mills so she could stay and nurse Malcolm and the seamstress back to health, even though they were in a perfectly good hospital. And she'd started making noises about Malcolm taking over the company again. If she managed to get in touch with the board of directors, she would soon find out he'd been telling them Malcolm was too busy sowing wild oats to be interested in running the company. It hadn't been difficult to convince them the handsome young man's interest centered on the

129

women under the clothing, not the clothing itself.

He took out his new gold pocket watch, engraved with the date of the *Titanic*'s sinking--a gift from the mayor's office--and checked the time. "Where are they, damn it? They should have been here by now." Eldon stood and scanned the room toward the tall gothic arches of the main entry. He had agreed to meet them near the ticket booth at two o'clock, and it was quarter past already. As he searched the throng he saw Malcolm, half a head taller than most of the crowd, shepherding his mother and the little seamstress through the crush. A porter pushed a cart with their luggage close behind. He only took a dozen steps before he heard a voice that stopped him dead in his tracks.

Chapter 20

Bree gawked at the beautiful ceiling soaring high above her head. Never had she seen anything like the massive building. Her neck already hurt from staring out the window at the skyscrapers as they drove through the city, and she turned in a circle trying to take everything in. Pink granite gleamed on the walls and columns.

Malcolm grabbed her elbow and pulled her out of the way as a loaded luggage cart lumbered past. "You'd better pay attention. There are a lot more people here than back home, I'll warrant."

"It's so beautiful, Malcolm. Such a magnificent building. Do you know how tall it is?" she asked in awe.

"The dome is one hundred fifty feet high. The columns alone are sixty feet. It's only two years old." Before he told her any more, shouts rang out from a far corner.

Bree couldn't see over the heads of the hundreds of people milling about, but she heard Malcolm swear under his breath.

Elizabeth heard as well. "Malcolm! Whatever set you off?"

"Come along, Mother, Miss Barry. I believe Eldon is over this way." He took each of them by an elbow and made his way to where the shouting continued.

* * * *

"You can't fool me, Mister High-and-Mighty. I saw what you did. You killed old Latimer, shot him clean through. An' here you are, lettin' everyone call you a hero. Hero, my ass. You're a murderer, you are, and a yellow-bellied coward to boot!"

Bree saw Eldon, staring down at a scrawny, roughly dressed man with ginger hair and no hat, who shook his finger under the taller man's nose. Eldon's furious expression changed subtly, almost like fear, as he realized the three of them were observing the argument.

Eldon drew himself up to his full height of well over six feet, and said loudly, "You're drunk. I don't know who you are, or why you're making such absurd accusations. I suggest you leave immediately and seek medical help. You're obviously ill. Otherwise, I will summon the police."

"Eldon, what's this about?" Elizabeth stepped near.

"It's nothing, my dear. Just an inebriated or mentally ill person who is quite delusional." He turned away, but the man grabbed his arm.

"You can lie to them, me bucko, but I knows better. I'm leavin', so I am. But I'm headed straight to the pier. And I'm gonna tell them what you did. If I can find Timmy, he'll tell 'em you paid him to get on the lifeboat. You won't be so high an' mighty when the coppers come for you."

Eldon whirled and grabbed the man by the ragged lapels of his coat. "Don't threaten me, you little weasel! If you think the police would believe your wild story, you truly are crazy. I'm a respected man, very well connected. I have nothing to fear from you. Now get out of my sight before the *coppers* come looking for *you*." He shoved the man so hard he fell on his backside and slid into the feet of some bystanders.

The redhead struggled to his knees as he snarled. "You'll be sorry, you will. Fred Dunby don't let no man push him around. Especially a liar and a killer. Just you wait." He gathered himself up and jerked his coat back down where it belonged. "You'll see," he muttered as he turned on his heel and stalked into the crowd.

The four of them stood awkwardly as the bystanders wandered off. Bree was thankful their train was announced and they hurried off to their boarding track. No one mentioned the stranger's accusations, but Bree wondered if there was anything to them.

* * * *

She forgot all about the redheaded man as she laid eyes on the ornately decorated private railcar connected to the end of the train. They entered from the observation platform on the rear and stepped straight into a hallway. Eldon and Elizabeth preceded them, turning into the first doorway and closing the carved wooden door. Bree quickly took Malcolm up on his offer to show her around the car as the sound of raised voices came from behind the closed portal. He opened the door to the second stateroom, his, then the third, assigned to her.

"How clever. A bed that folds down off the wall. I'm sure it'll be quite cozy and comfortable with the chair and picture window." Bree brushed past him and turned around in the middle of the room, admiring the watered silk wallpaper and plush Aubusson carpet.

Malcolm laughed. "It feels comfortable now, but with the bed down there's hardly room to turn around." He motioned to a narrow door on the wall. "The powder room is through there. There is a larger bathing chamber next door, which we all share."

He led her into the corridor and farther down the car. They passed a neat and compact galley where a white-haired black man put packages into cupboards.

"Hello, Peter. Good to see you again," Malcolm said as the man turned from his duties.

The dark face split into a wide grin, showing large white teeth. "Good day to you, Mr. Malcolm. Things haven't been the same with you gone. I got your favorites in here." Peter nodded toward the cupboard.

Malcolm chuckled and said, "I can't wait. This is Miss Barry. She's traveling up to The Dell with us."

"Afternoon, miss. You need anything, you let me know."

Bree smiled. "Thank you. I can't imagine what could be missing from this magnificent train. I've never seen anything like it." Peter smiled proprietarily and went back to work.

Malcolm took her elbow and guided her into the lounge. The other rooms were richly appointed with heavy carved wood, patterned tin ceiling and thick carpets, but the lounge was far grander. A marble-mantled fireplace abutted the wall adjacent to the galley.

One front corner of the car sported a baby grand piano, and elegant chandeliers hung from the coffered ceiling. Comfortable-looking sofas and chairs were scattered around the room in casual groupings while Oriental rugs covered the polished wood floor. In the corner near the galley sat an inlaid dining table and six chairs. Large picture windows filled almost all the wall space.

Bree gazed out one of the velvet-flanked windows and watched the crowds milling about on the platform. Before she turned away, she noticed the russet-haired man staring directly at her. She sucked in her breath, her hand grasping the cross she always wore.

"What is it?" Malcolm asked, seeing her expression.

"That man, the one your stepfather argued with. He's out there. He was staring right at me."

He strode to the window. "Where?"

She stepped up beside him. "There, by the column." She searched in vain for the bright thatch of hair. "He's not there now. I know I saw him, truly I did."

Malcolm frowned. "I'm sure you did. He probably followed us. Whatever is going on between him and Eldon doesn't appear settled yet."

A knock on the front door caused Bree to jerk in surprise. The portal opened and the conductor stuck his head in. "Leavin' in a moment, folks. Everyone aboard?"

"Yes, thanks. We're all set."

The man tipped his hat and retreated. A short time later, they heard a clank and felt a hard tug, followed by squealing wheels and

135

the sensation of slow, jarring movements.

Bree staggered and fell into Malcolm's chest. He caught her, holding her tightly to his rock-hard body for a moment. His hands slid from her shoulders down to her wrists before he slowly stepped back, keeping a grip on her hands. She bit her lip and looked away, shocked at how her heart beat faster as he held her. And wishing for another jerk to send her back into his arms.

"Bree."

She gazed up at him, the serious tone a far cry from the casual banter he usually used. His deep blue eyes glittered with emotion as they bored into hers. There was an intensity in his whole being that excited and frightened her at the same time. He took a step forward, and she tipped her head up to see his face. His hands returned to her arms, sliding up and down gently, then snaked around her back. She held her breath. His head bent down and she caught a whiff of his spicy cologne. As his warm lips touched hers, she melted against him, and his arms tightened. She didn't know how long the embrace went on, but a sudden loud cough brought them back to the real world. Malcolm's arms dropped, and they whirled around to see a smirking Eldon leaning casually on a dining chair.

"Well, well. This is a surprise. The innocent little seamstress and the rich playboy. Could there be a more clichéd scenario? Be careful, my dear. Our Malcolm has quite a reputation with the ladies. Elizabeth might not appreciate the two of you carrying on right under her nose, either." Eldon's sneering tone brought a burning flush to Bree's face.

"Shut up, Eldon," Malcolm snapped.

Bree stared at him, surprised at his furious tone.

Eldon took a stride toward them, his fists bunched, but before he crossed the swaying room, Elizabeth stepped out of the corridor. "What's the matter? Malcolm, what's going on?"

"Nothing, Mother. Eldon seems to think I'm trying to seduce your seamstress. I was about to explain what I feel for Bree is none of his business, and I've never considered her the menial servant he does. Now, if you will excuse us, I'll escort Bree to her stateroom so she can freshen up."

He took Bree's numb arm and headed toward the rear of the car, brushing hard against Eldon, who was knocked to the side when he refused to give way. Bree dropped her eyes, mortified, as they passed Elizabeth.

Malcolm paused at the doorway to her room. She would have left him there, but he gently pushed her inside, followed, and shut the door. She gasped. Surely he didn't think he could accost her--and that she would allow it--after being so embarrassed?

She opened her mouth to give him a piece of her mind, but he pressed his index finger to her lips, halting her tirade.

"Bree, wait. I know what you think. It's not true. Eldon said what he did to get this exact reaction. He wants to upset you, anger me, humiliate us both. Don't let him do it. I'm not sorry, or ashamed, by what happened between us. As a matter of fact, I've been praying for the opportunity for days." She started to protest and he shook his head.

"Hear me out. I know you think me a cad. A rich playboy like Eldon said. But it's not true, at least not since the day I first met you. When you were ill and I thought I would lose you, I wished I'd gone to the bottom of the sea on that damn ship. And when you got better, I couldn't wait to tell you how I felt. I didn't intend it to be in quite this manner, but I don't care. I've fallen in love with you, Bree. You have more life in your little finger than any ten women I've ever known in my life. Don't let him run you off. Because I'll have to keep coming after you. Please."

Bree was speechless. *He said he loves me. Gu sealladh orm!* She searched his eyes, and saw no sign of jest, just an incredibly intense, hopeful stare. She reached up and laid her hand against his cheek. His eyes closed as he turned and nuzzled her palm. She was overwhelmed with emotion and felt tears well. Malcolm's sapphire eyes opened and, in a quick movement, he pulled her close. His mouth descended. Her lashes lowered as she reveled in the taste of his lips, the feel of his hands sliding up and down her back, the pressure of his firm chest against her tender breasts. It was heaven.

When he finally raised his head she clung to him, not at all sure her knees would hold her up. He didn't seem to mind.

Blue eyes stared deeply into hers. "Bree, marry me."

Her legs did give out and only his strong grip kept her from falling. He bent and slipped an arm under her knees, picking her up and carrying her to the overstuffed chair in the corner. He sank into it with her in his lap, her cheek against his shoulder, palm resting over his heart. She felt it beating very fast, and knew hers did the same.

138

Bree tipped her head back and looked up. He stared down at her, his expression somber.

"Marry you? We hardly know each other, Malcolm, *a ghaoil.*"

"What does that mean? It's beautiful, like you."

She hesitated. Did she mean it? Could she possibly love a man she'd only known a few weeks? Yes. The answer came to her so quickly and so clearly there was no room for doubt. "It means 'my love'. And yes. If you truly want to marry me, yes."

Malcolm threw his head back and howled like a wolf, then leaned down and kissed her very thoroughly. Bree shivered as his tongue slid along her lips, probing, then slipped inside to play. It was such a strange sensation, but she tentatively reciprocated.

At her response, his arms tightened and Malcolm twisted in the seat a fraction so her hip rested fully in his lap. She felt the heat of him through her clothing. Bree's eyes opened wide as she became aware of the hard length pressing against her.

Malcolm sensed her growing consternation and cupped her face gently with his hand. "I won't hurt you. I can't help wanting you, but I'll never push you." He bent down and kissed her again. His touch was so tender her fears instantly melted away. Light as a feather, his hand slid up her arm to rest at her neck, his thumb brushing the soft niche under her ear. Malcolm's other hand slipped around her waist. As his kiss deepened, a delicious warmth spread from her center. Her arm was pinned between them, his heartbeat reverberating through her. She looped her free arm around his neck, fingers twining in the curls at his collar. Through her gown, the heat from Malcolm's hand

139

seemed to brand her. His thumb stroked back and forth across her ribs a mere inch from her breast. She sighed, or was it a moan of pleasure? Bree wasn't sure.

His wayward hand slipped up to her breast, his thumb grazing her nipple, which blossomed until it puckered her gown. Mouth slanted, his lips pressed down with a feverish urgency as his hand slipped into the bodice and slowly nudged the fabric off her shoulder.

Bree's eyelids fluttered at the sudden spasm of passion that threatened to burst her into pieces. Malcolm's lips pressed warm kisses from the corner of her mouth, down her neck, lingering on her collarbone before slipping lower. As his tongue licked at her nipple, Bree gasped in shock. The heat of his mouth closing over the swollen bud drove her mad. She felt a sudden wetness between her thighs. All these sensations were so new, so powerful. She placed a shaking hand against his chest and pushed.

"Please, you must stop. I...I...don't know what..." Her body cried out for more, but her mind urged caution against the multitude of strange, exciting sensations.

Malcolm allowed her to push him away with only a small groan. He bent and kissed her on the forehead then sighed deeply and leaned back to look at her, his grin lopsided. "You're right about that. I must stop or prove Eldon only too right. But it's just until we're wed, my love. Then, I intend to start again. And again. And again."

They turned at a soft knock from the door. This time there was no start of guilt. No embarrassment.

Elizabeth called, "Bree, dear? Peter says he'll have hors d' oeuvres ready shortly. Will you join us, please?"

Bree slipped off Malcolm's lap and quickly adjusted her gown, still feeling the imprint of Malcolm's lip on the sensitive nub. As she would have stepped away from him, he caught her hand and kept her close. He stood and opened the door. "Come in, Mother. We'd like to speak with you a moment. Privately."

If Elizabeth was surprised to find her son in the seamstress' room she hid it well, grasping Bree's hands and apologizing, "My dear, I'm so sorry. Eldon had no right to say what he did. We had quite a row about it just now."

Malcolm gently cut her off. "Mother, don't worry. We don't care what Eldon has to say. What matters is I've asked Bree to marry me, and she's accepted. I hope you approve, but even if you don't, I know you'll be too gracious to act as he did."

Elizabeth's gray eyes widened and her gaze flicked back and forth between them. Bree held her breath.

The older woman's chin raised and her face took on a thoughtful expression. Then she gave a quick nod as a broad smile spread over her face. Elizabeth stepped forward, enfolded Bree in her arms and planted a light kiss to her temple. "I told you I always wished for a daughter, dear. Now I'll have one." She released Bree and pulled Malcolm's head down to kiss his cheek. "Congratulations, my boy. I've had moments I worried about you, but not now. I think you'll be fine. Oh, this is wonderful. A wedding. I've never planned a wedding! Percy's mother made all the arrangements when we married, and Eldon insisted on a small service at the chapel near The

Dell. I'm so excited. Come on, you two. We're going to open a split of Champagne--or two--and toast the occasion. And I assure you, Eldon *will* behave himself." From the look in her future mother-in-law's eye, Bree thought he'd better, if he knew what was good for him.

The three of them made their way back to the lounge and Elizabeth announced to Eldon he would soon be a stepfather-in-law. He choked on his whiskey and soda, but wisely nodded and said, "I suppose congratulations are in order. You chose a lovely young lady for your bride, Malcolm. I'm sure the two of you will be very happy."

Bree noted Eldon's white-knuckled grip around his glass and the way his smile didn't reach his eyes, and knew the man held back furious anger. She took a step closer to Malcolm, comforted when he immediately slipped his arm around her and pulled her securely against his shoulder.

Eldon sat in the background drinking the rest of the night while they made wedding plans. When Bree yawned widely and made embarrassed apologies, Elizabeth shooed the younger pair off to bed. Eldon declined to follow, saying he wasn't tired.

Elizabeth walked ahead of them, stopping at Bree's door. She turned and hugged her future daughter-in-law, kissed her on the forehead and said, "I'm so happy, my dear. Truly."

"And perhaps a bit surprised?" Malcolm teased.

"Well, yes, maybe a little. But only for a moment. Now, it's been a busy day and I don't want either of you falling ill again." She gave him a knowing smile and went to her room.

"What she means is she expects us in our respective rooms in the very near future." Their gazes met and he bent down for a long, tender kiss. Malcolm straightened and groaned. "I hope you two get this wedding put together soon, because walking away from you is getting harder by the moment."

Bree giggled, stood on her tiptoes and brought his face back down for another quick kiss. "Good night, Malcolm," she whispered and slipped into her room.

She closed the door and leaned back, eyes closed, and murmured, "*Caidil gu math, caomh.*" She danced across the room, twirling, and flung herself into the chair. As she stared at the elaborate tin ceiling, she marveled at the changes in her life. A few weeks ago, she was essentially a slave to her family and the Rothberrys. After nearly dying on the *Titanic*, she was betrothed to an incredibly handsome, loving man, and had gained a dear new friend in Elizabeth. She reached up, touched the cross and closed her eyes. "Thank you." Bree felt as if she were floating on a cloud as she quickly prepared for bed and climbed into the fold-down berth, which Peter had made up for her while they celebrated. The mattress was a bit hard, but the soft pillow and monogrammed sheets were more comfortable than any bedding she'd ever experienced. The cashmere blanket felt light as a feather. She turned down the gaslight and burrowed in, soothed by the repetitive clickety-clack of the train's wheels. An exhausted sleep overcame her almost immediately.

* * * *

Eldon poured another stiff drink and plopped down on the sofa, not caring if his dirty boots left a smear across the fine fabric. This had been a trying day. First, in a city of more than a million people, he managed to run into one of the dozen men who knew how he really got off the damn ship. Of course the police would never believe the man, not over the word of a DuMont. *But what if they talked to more of the crewmen from the lifeboat?* And there was always the possibility someone had seen him with the steward, Timmy, and Peterson. Some bleeding heart would probably make a big deal about the death of a drunken sot and a servant, and he'd find himself having to defend his actions. Any fool could see it was the only way he could have gotten off the ship, and of the three, he was certainly the most valuable.

He swirled the amber liquid in the heavy cut glass tumbler. Good thing he was on his way out of the city. The chances of running into any of the crewmen in Linton were negligible. The police up there knew which side their bread was buttered on as well. They wouldn't risk upsetting Elizabeth with wild accusations.

He relaxed. There wasn't anything to worry about, not really. He'd stick close to home for a while, make sure no problems came up then get back to business. He *was* disappointed with the seamstress, though. She'd had potential, until she managed to snag Malcolm. It would have been interesting to see how long it took for her to switch her loyalties from Elizabeth to him. Ah, well, there were other diversions available. One woman was the same as the other, especially in the dark.

Chapter 21

The next day passed quickly as the train rumbled across the countryside and made stops at several towns. Their car was uncoupled from one train and added to another two times before the conductor knocked at the door and said they were approaching Linton.

Malcolm went down the hall with Bree and helped gather her few belongings.

"Is it far to your home?" she asked as they stepped into the corridor.

Malcolm hefted her bags and took them back to the observation platform to set them with the others. "No. The car will be waiting for us at the station, and it's only another thirty minutes or so to the house."

* * * *

Bree sat on a sofa in the lounge, positioned so she could see out one of the big windows. The train slowed to a crawl, jerking and creaking as it approached a rustic train station. A large, sleek Rolls

Royce, the pearly silver paint polished to a high sheen, idled next to the siding. A uniformed chauffeur stood at attention, one hand resting next to the elegant silver lady hood ornament. The heavily wooded area surrounding the station prevented her from seeing anything beyond the building.

She felt a soft touch on her shoulder and turned around. Malcolm smiled down at her. "Ready?"

Bree returned the smile, stood and arranged the folds of her new dove-gray outfit. He took her arm and escorted her out onto the platform, preceding her down the steps before he turned to give her a hand. A stiffly silent Eldon and Elizabeth were close behind.

The chauffeur, introduced as Carlisle, efficiently loaded the baggage in the huge trunk while they settled into the roomy sedan. Moments later, they were motoring down a dirt road.

"I'll be dropping you at the house, Elizabeth. I've been gone far too long. I need to get back to my office and see what needs to be done," Eldon said, staring out the window.

"Right now? Surely nothing can be done today that couldn't wait until tomorrow?" Elizabeth protested.

He stared at her, his expression stony. "That's why *I* run the company, dear. You never seem to realize how important it is to have a firm hand on the reins. Left to you, the employees would be allowed to run the company into the ground."

Bree felt Malcolm tense beside her. "You know, Eldon, I discussed that very thing with Mother. We believe it's time I stepped up and took the burden of running the company off your hands.

146

You've given up so many of your leisure activities, and it's taken you away from your duties as Mother's husband. If you're going in today, you can instruct the accounting department to get the books ready for me to review. I'll also want to have a meeting with all the supervisors this week. After seeing the designs in Europe, we'll need to get started on our plans for next year's line right away."

As Malcolm spoke, Bree saw Eldon's jaw set and his eyes narrow. He canted his head and in a lecturing tone replied, "Well, now. That's an ambitious plan, my boy. But I think you've forgotten we answer to a board of directors, and you have no experience in running a company of this size. If I let you waltz in and starting making changes, you could bring the whole company crashing down. No. I think you'd best let me sit down with the board and try to convince them you're ready to start taking on more work." Eldon smiled, but his eyes stayed hard. "Besides, you should spend time with your new fiancée. These sudden romances are so fragile, you know. Why, with you gone all the time, she might find her interests wandering."

Bree gasped and opened her mouth to protest. A gentle squeeze of her hand caused her to look up into Malcolm's deep blue eyes. He smiled down at her and said, "Bree's fidelity is uncontested, Eldon." His gaze hardened as he surveyed his father-in-law. "Yours, however, is. I'll be at the office tomorrow, and every day, so you might as well get used to it. The company has been mine since I reached my majority. I've allowed you to make it into something different from what my father wanted, and I intend to remedy that forthwith. You can go along for the ride, or you can get off the gravy train--it's no matter to me."

Before the argument flared, the car pulled into a large cobbled circular drive and rolled to a stop before a pair of tall double doors.

Further conversation was put aside as Malcolm and the butler, Anderson, spent the next few minutes getting luggage deposited in the house. Elizabeth escorted Bree upstairs to her room, located on the inside of one wing of the U-shaped house. Floor-to-ceiling windows gave view across a garden full of riotous color to the other wing. Manicured lawns flowed over gently curving hillocks topped with trimmed topiaries. Hedges boxed in formal rose and herb gardens. Bree couldn't wait to stroll down the gravel pathways.

"It's lovely, Elizabeth," she marveled.

She turned and surveyed the large bedroom. Gray watered-silk fabric covered the walls, and heavy gray-and-rose-striped damask drapes flanked the windows and dripped from a half-circle over the head of the bed. Massive furniture, polished to a deep shine, spoke of careful attention. A carved set of steps sat next to the tall poster, and Bree knew she would need them.

A clatter outside the door distracted her and she stood back as a man brought in her baggage, followed by a maid who immediately began opening the bags and sorting the clothing. Bree stepped forward. "Please, you don't need to do that. I can put everything away."

The maid looked inquiringly at Elizabeth, who nodded. The servants padded silently out.

"It's a beautiful room. I'm so very grateful for the opportunity to stay here," Bree said.

"Nonsense. I'm the grateful one. If not for you, I surely would have died on that ship."

"And I in the water," Bree reminded her, and they both laughed.

Elizabeth walked toward the door. "I'll leave you to get settled. The bathing chamber is through that door, and we'll have a late tea downstairs when you're ready." She left the room, her gown swishing softly.

Bree unpacked. Even with all the new clothing, the dresser and closet were nearly bare when she finished. She stopped a moment to admire the lovely gowns lined up on their hangers. After spending years creating clothing for Lady Rothberry, she was amazed to have such finery of her very own. "I'll pay her back for every last one," she vowed quietly.

Chapter 22

Bree descended the wide staircase, letting her hand slide down the smooth, polished handrail. She admired the intricately carved floral panels holding it up. The house was very well cared for and decorated with great skill. The colors were muted; a soft sage green, dusty rose and cream interspersed with touches of gold and black. The honey-hued parquet floor contrasted nicely with the darker wood trim. Prisms of light sparkled on the walls from sunlight glinting off a large crystal chandelier centered over the foyer. When she first entered the house, she'd been so busy watching where she was going, she hadn't had time to admire the vast room. If the rest of the house was finished in the same style, it would truly be a grand home.

Laughter and conversation from a room to the left of the stair trickled into the foyer. She made her way to the broad doorway and peeked in. She lost track of time as she listened to Malcolm and Elizabeth talking and laughing together. How wonderful it must be to have a family able to sit together and laugh, and talk about all manner of things.

"Come in, my dear," Elizabeth called as she noticed Bree.

Malcolm sat across from his mother on a short settee, while Elizabeth occupied a big wing-back chair. The room carried the same color scheme as the foyer. Floor-to-ceiling windows at the back of the room let in light and provided a close-up view of the same gardens Bree's room overlooked.

Malcolm stood and stepped toward her with a smile. He took her arm and led her to the settee. The size of the seat required their sides rest snuggly together as he laid his arm along the seatback, his hand resting against her neck. She smiled up at him tentatively and was rewarded with a gentle squeeze of her shoulder.

Bree relaxed back into the seat and decided it was just where she wanted to be.

"Are you comfortable in your room, love?" he asked.

The endearment sent shivers down her spine. "It's wonderful. Lady Rothberry would hate the whole house. It makes hers look like a moldy farmhouse in comparison. And the colors are perfect."

Malcolm glanced at his mother and nodded. "Mother has an eye for colors and fabrics, which is why Father enjoyed her collaboration. The two of them would come up with our fashion designs all by themselves. Even after seeing the French couturiers, I don't think any of them have as much talent as she does."

Elizabeth colored at her son's compliment. "Malcolm, you do exaggerate. I was thrilled to see the new season's designs. All I can do is make an attempt to copy them for our own clothing. I'll never be that good."

Malcolm shook his head and looked serious. "Don't sell yourself short, Mother. I'll bet your sketch book was filled with new, improved versions of what you saw there. It's too bad it rests on the bottom of the North Atlantic." He explained to Bree, "Mother is an excellent artist. She can sketch a dress faster than anyone I've ever seen. I'll take you to the office with me later and show you some of her sketch books."

"I would love to see them."

"Bree, dear, didn't you design the gowns for your employer?" Elizabeth asked.

"Yes, but Lady Rothberry was a woman of very limited taste. All her dresses were of the same style. I barely got away with changing trim and tiny details. Anything else and she would not accept it."

"We must work together, then. It will be such fun to discuss my designs with another woman."

"I would be honored to make patterns and sew for you," Bree said, excited to think she might have a hand in real design work.

From then on the conversation centered around clothing--from type of cloth to colors, cuts, trims and lengths. When the women began discussing finer details, Malcolm stood and announced, "You two seem to have the situation well in hand. I think I'll take a ride on old Soldier. He's probably gotten fat and lazy since I've been gone, and I know I could use the exercise. I won't be long."

Bree watched with admiration as he strode out of the room.

Elizabeth laughed and repeated her question again, drawing Bree's attention from the now-empty foyer. "Don't worry, my dear.

You'll see so much of the boy you'll find yourself glad for a few moments alone now and again."

Bree shook her head. "I don't think so. I really don't."

They sat in the sunny room, sipping tea and discussing fashion throughout the afternoon. The sun had sunk behind a low hill by the time a maid appeared in the doorway.

"Cook says to ask when you'd be wantin' dinner, ma'am?"

Elizabeth looked up at the mantel clock. "Tell her to plan on seven o'clock. Malcolm has gone riding and Eldon has not yet returned from town."

"Very good, ma'am." The girl made a brief curtsy and disappeared.

At the mention of Eldon's name, Elizabeth seemed to grow restless and got up. She strolled to the wall of windows and pushed a latch. Bree was surprised to see one of the windows open like a door. The latch was concealed in a wooden rosette that blended into the carved design of the massive twelve-foot-tall door. The sound of birds warbling and insects humming drifted into the room with an early evening breeze. Elizabeth was pensive and Bree stood and walked over to her.

"What is it? You seem worried," Bree asked.

"I've been thinking about how much I missed it here and wondering what the next few months will bring. Early this year there was trouble. The government reduced the hours worked by women and children in the mills. Percy spearheaded the legislation but after he died, no one thought to explain the plan to the workers before it

153

went into effect. Then Eldon apparently forgot to tell the bookkeeper to increase the wages to keep their paychecks the same, at least he said he forgot. When they got their pay and saw it was less than they were used to, they held a strike. The mill owners tried to force the women back to work. It got so ugly that the workers tried to send their children away to keep them safe. Someone, Malcolm thinks Eldon, called in hired thugs to prevent the children from getting on the trains. The men behaved horribly, beating the women and even some children, then took the women to jail. I couldn't find Eldon so I went down to the police station and made them let everyone go. Of course Eldon was furious. He said I should have stayed out of business decisions, but by then it was too late." Elizabeth turned away. "That was the first time he struck me. He'll be livid now Malcolm is stepping in to manage the company."

Bree reached out and laid her hand on the older woman's arm. "You don't have to talk about it if you don't want to, but I really do know what it was like for you."

Elizabeth sighed heavily. "He's right to blame me. I'm foolish to think I can manage the business. I shouldn't meddle."

"Those are his words, aren't they?" Bree asked softly.

Elizabeth's mouth turned up in a hint of a smile. "You *do* know. Yes, to begin with, they were his words. Sometimes I can't help but believe them. It's been so awful. I didn't want anyone to know, especially Malcolm."

Bree nodded. "I understand, because I watched the same thing happen to my mother. I don't know how it was when they first

154

married, but for as long as I can remember my father beat my mother, nearly every day. I listened to her pleas for mercy. I heard him tell her she was stupid, or clumsy, or ugly so many times. At first I thought every family acted like that, but then I went to school and found out it wasn't true. That wasn't love. My mother was smart too, and very talented. She was good and kind and pretty once. He took it all away and turned her into a shell of a person. I think when she realized she was dying she was glad, because she knew it would be over. I couldn't help her because I was too young, and then it was too late. When I saw you that first day, even though I'd never met you or your husband before, somehow I knew." She fell silent.

In a small voice Elizabeth said, "Eldon wasn't always like this. He was so very solicitous when we were courting and for months after we married. After that first time, it happened more often. Once, at a party, he heard someone asked me about a bruise. It didn't stop him, but he was very careful to make sure he didn't leave marks anyone could see. I know I'm not to blame, but when he's there, shouting at me, I can't think what to say."

"I know." Bree grasped Elizabeth's hand and gave it a sympathetic squeeze.

Chapter 23

Malcolm limped in an hour after he was expected. He knew his mother would be fretting about dinner being ruined. He had intended to sneak in, change his clothing, and wash the blood from his face before appearing before Bree and his mother. But old Murray from the stable saw him and made a beeline for the kitchen. The whole house would know something happened within minutes. He didn't want Bree and his mother to find out from a servant.

He glanced at the parlor doorway and saw Bree's smile die, replaced by a look of horror. She ran toward him, Elizabeth right on her heels.

"Malcolm!" she cried.

He held up a hand and shook his head. "It's not as bad as it appears. I'm fine." The look on his future wife's face told him she begged to differ.

"But what happened?" Elizabeth asked.

Malcolm's shoulders slumped and he hung his head. "Someone shot Soldier." Shocked gasps greeted his harsh statement. Before either woman could ask the multitude of questions he saw in their eyes, he said, "Please. Give me a moment to clean up and change. I'll be right back down to tell you the whole story. Mother, dear, perhaps you'd have Anderson bring a stiff whiskey and soda to my room." He smiled reassuringly and slowly made his way up the stairs to his room, suppressing a groan of pain to keep up the pretense.

The women sat pensively in the parlor as he returned a quarter of an hour later. Another glass amply filled with caramel-colored liquor sat on the table, a soda siphon and tall cut glass decanter on a tray ready for a refill. He took a hefty slug of the drink, closing his eyes as it burned its way to his stomach. Knowing he couldn't put it off any longer, he sat and snuggled a pale-faced Bree close.

"I rode the north trail."

Elizabeth nodded.

"By the time I heard the shot, Soldier was already going down. I was lucky. We were steps away from the creek. I ended up in a patch of moss, instead of coming down on jagged granite. Other than a few bruises and some scratches, I'm fine. Soldier's gone, though."

"Oh, son, I'm so sorry." Elizabeth turned to Bree and explained, "He raised that horse from a colt. I remember him sitting up all night with Murray the night old Soldier was born."

Bree turned to Malcolm, "But who shot at you?"

"That's something I intend to find out. I'll talk to Murray after dinner and have him put the word out. If anyone was hunting in the woods, the men will find out."

"You need to talk to Ernie too," his mother added.

As Bree raised a questioning eyebrow, Malcolm explained, "Ernie Fletcher is the chief of police in Linton. I've known him all my life. He grew up with my father and Eldon." He turned to Elizabeth. "It will wait until tomorrow. Now, is dinner totally ruined, or do you think we have a chance?"

He could tell his mother was annoyed by his cavalier attitude as she stood and led the way to the dining room.

After dinner, Malcolm suggested he take Bree on a moonlight tour of the gardens. As they slowly meandered the paths, he asked her about her childhood and home, pointedly avoiding any discussion about his accident. Bree played along, described the emerald green hills and dells, and the lonely sound of waves crashing on shore during winter storms. She told him about the Rothberrys and their manor house. He drew her closer, jaw flexing, as she averted her eyes and gave him a brief recap of the disgusting suggestions the lord made the night before she escaped to the *Titanic*. His mouth turned down at the corners as she haltingly spoke about the small cottage she called home and the death of her mother. Much as he wanted to know what kind of family produced such an exceptional daughter, he accepted it would take time before he knew everything about her, just as it would for her to learn about him. Well, they had a lifetime ahead of them, didn't they?

"It was an accident today, wasn't it Malcolm?" Bree suddenly asked, unable to ignore his limping progress.

"Of course. Why would you think anything else?" Malcolm had his own doubts whether it was an accident but didn't want to frighten

Bree or his mother. He fully intended to do some serious investigation to find out exactly what happened. And why.

"No reason, I guess."

She was very subdued the rest of the evening and, as he escorted her up to her room, he suggested, "Come to town with me tomorrow. I'll show you around and introduce you to some of our friends and employees. And we need to talk to Mother about an engagement party. I want to make sure everyone knows you're already spoken for."

"I'd like that very much, but right now I'd like something else even more." She gazed up at him, eyes bright, lips puckered.

Desire flared in his groin as he obliged, bending down and pressing his lips to hers. Bree's body melted against him. She tasted like the cherry cordial his mother served after dinner. He pulled her closer, his mouth welded to hers with an increasing heat. He felt her sigh against his lips. Hands shaking, he pulled back and looked down at her pale face. Her eyes flickered open, like she awakened from a dream. He saw a faint tremble in her rose-hued lips. She blinked, her green eyes glazed with longing.

"Was that what you had in mind?" he teased to diffuse the sensual tension.

An impish smile touched her face. "It'll do in a pinch," she said as she skipped though the doorway.

"I'll give you a pinch, you little vixen." But before he could pursue her, Bree slammed the door shut. He heard her amused giggle from the other side.

"Goodnight, my love," she called.

Malcolm answered in kind and, shaking his head at her antics, made his way to his room.

As he readied for bed he was made aware of a myriad damaged muscles from his fall. By morning, he'd be lucky if he could get out of bed.

He lay down, hands behind his head, thinking over the events right before Soldier went down. They'd been cantering casually along a well-known trail. The track narrowed as it passed between a huge old pine and the steep slope where the creek cut away the bank. The shot caught Soldier dead on his chest, and he'd probably taken only a step or two more before going down on his forelegs and tumbling over the bank. Malcolm mused, "Anywhere but the bed of moss and I'd likely have broken my neck. No one would have heard me cry out, unless they were right there on the trail." If none of the locals admitted to hunting deer out of season, he would ask Ernie to check on visitors from out of the area. The unwelcome thought that the shooter might have been hunting something besides deer niggled around in his head, and it was a long time before he found sleep.

Chapter 24

The next morning Bree and Elizabeth enjoyed an early breakfast. Neither Eldon nor Malcolm joined them. Elizabeth had no idea where Eldon was, but that didn't appear to be an unusual situation. Malcolm, they'd been informed by Anderson, had breakfasted in his room before enjoying a hot bath to soak away some of the stiffness. He was due to join them momentarily.

While they waited in the parlor, Elizabeth gave in to Bree's request and fetched a large sketch pad from her room. It contained her sketches from the previous season. As the pages turned, Bree was awed by the detailed, flowing drawings of the couturier's models in their finery. The sketches gave the impression of movement and grace. Next to many of the pictures were neat notes suggesting changes to the design.

"I see what Malcolm means, Elizabeth. Your ideas would greatly improve the designs. You're a wonderful artist. Do you paint as well?"

She nodded. "But I haven't in years. Percy used to take me for drives. If there was something interesting, we'd stop and I'd sketch. If there was time, I'd paint. Eldon never has the time, and I don't seem to have the interest anymore." Elizabeth nodded toward a writing desk in the corner. "That was the last painting I did."

A small, framed oil of a country lane flanked by brilliantly colored fall foliage hung over the desk. The woods seemed to be afire with color. "Oh, Elizabeth," Bree said as she walked over and stood close to the painting, "it's wonderful. I almost expect to see a coach and four drive up the road."

Elizabeth laughed shyly.

They both heard Malcolm's footsteps on the stair and met him at the bottom. "How are you feeling, son?" Elizabeth asked.

"Just a bit stiff. I'm sure I'll get it worked out shortly." He smiled at Bree. "Ready for your tour, Miss Barry?"

She grinned. "At your pleasure, Mr. DuMont." Bree blushed as a devilish look entered his eye at the word *pleasure* and hoped Elizabeth hadn't noticed.

If she had, she gave no sign. "Have fun, you two. Dinner will be at seven, as usual." She started to turn away then paused. "Be careful, Malcolm."

He nodded. "Always."

Bree shivered with a strange foreboding, but the feeling slipped away in the wake of Malcolm's boyish enthusiasm as he helped her into a small, clever-looking white automobile.

"How quaint."

Malcolm put his hands on hips, pretending to be outraged. "It's not quaint. It's a racecar. A Mercer Type Thirty-Five Raceabout, to be exact. It's been clocked at nearly a hundred miles an hour."

"Oooh." Bree tried to act suitably impressed, but he obviously exaggerated. Nothing on earth could go that fast. It *was* cute, though. White paint accented by narrow black stripes shone in the sun, and the bright red leather seats were deeply padded. She frowned as she noticed the windscreen was only a round piece of glass attached in front of the steering wheel. Concerned, she asked, "Do you have a lot of bugs here?"

He was confused for a moment, then realized what she talked about and chuckled. "A few. I promise I won't go fast. At least not until we get you a driving uniform and goggles."

He helped her settle into the snug seat, tucking her skirts in. She watched with interest as he went through several steps to start the car. He finally turned the crank, fiddled some more, and they were off. He was true to his word, and the little car jounced along at a sedate pace. The breeze still whipped the pins from her hair and it twisted and whirled behind her. By the time they arrived in the small hamlet of Linton, her hair was a tangled mass, spilling over her shoulders and down her back in mad profusion.

Bree caught a glimpse of herself in the plate glass window and moaned. "Oh, dear. Look at me." She tried to gather the recalcitrant tendrils and force them into submission, but curls kept escaping.

"I like it loose. It's such a striking color and with all those curls, it shouldn't be forced into some staid bun." Malcolm flicked a tendril and watched it twine around his wrist. At her dubious expression, he shook his head and stepped behind her. With a few deft turns of his wrist, he tied his cravat around the mass of auburn tresses at the base of her neck, letting curls tumble freely down her back to her waist. "There. All fixed."

Bree turned back to the window and shook her head. "I'm a mess. I can't be out in public like this."

He raised an eyebrow and grinned. "So you're saying I should take you somewhere private?"

She slapped him playfully on the arm. "Oh, you. I was promised a tour, and I guess I'll have to look like something the cat dragged in until we get back to the house."

Malcolm bent to her ear and murmured, "My cat never dragged in anything as delectable as you."

Bree twisted her head around and gazed into his face. His lips were lowering to hers when a strident voice rang out.

Chapter 25

"Malcolm? Malcolm DuMont, it is you! Why, it's been ages, darling. And who is this child--some niece I've never met?"

Bree stared at the exquisitely beautiful blonde woman. She was dressed to perfection in a royal blue suit, topped with a huge straw boater. A fine gauzy veil drew attention to her almond-shaped amber eyes.

Malcolm straightened slowly. Bree wasn't sure what his expression reflected. It could have been disappointment or perhaps impatience, but he responded, "Hello, Melody. You're looking well."

The woman advanced on Malcolm, nudging Bree aside before she rose on tiptoe to plant a lingering kiss on Malcolm's lips. Bree's eyes widened. As Melody stepped back, Malcolm glanced down at Bree. He grimaced uncomfortably and shrugged. She raised her chin, one eyebrow arched high.

"Erm... Melody, this is Bree Barry, my fiancée. Bree this is--" A loud gasp interrupted his introduction.

"Your fiancée! Why Malcolm DuMont, you cad. You left here

after giving me the distinct impression *I* was your fiancée. I've been making plans all this time, waiting for you to return and set the date. How could you!"

Bree took a step away and regarded Malcolm, eyes wide.

He held his hands out and said, "Now, Melody, you know we never discussed any such thing. I told you in no uncertain terms I wasn't ready to consider marriage to you or anyone else. If you harbored any false hopes, they were of your own making." Malcolm stepped around the sputtering blonde and put his arm around Bree. "I hope you will welcome my future wife to the community with the same gracious manner I've always seen in you."

Bree scrutinized Malcolm's face, searching for the truth. How could Melody and Malcolm each be so sure about something so completely different? Certainly you would know if you were engaged?

Melody's mouth shut with an audible snap and her gaze shifted from Malcolm to Bree and back several times. She blinked and took a deep breath. "Of course, Malcolm." She turned to Bree and spoke slowly and clearly as if speaking to a child, "Hello, there. I'm Melody Parsons. Malcolm and I have known each other all our lives. Welcome." She stuck out her gloved hand and when Bree did the same, grasped the tips of Bree's fingers and gave a tiny squeeze, letting go immediately.

Melody immediately turned back to Malcolm. "Are you sure her parents will approve a marriage at such a young age, Malcolm dear?" Her mouth made a moue. "I mean really, Malcolm, I never thought of

166

you as a cradle robber."

The hackles on the back of Bree's neck rose and she narrowed her eyes as she contemplated the best way to deal with the irritating woman. Malcolm stepped between them.

"Melody, Bree is quite fully of age. Though I expect her youthful beauty will put all others to shame even in her dotage, which I sincerely hope to see."

The blonde had a momentary blank look as if trying to discern an insult in his statement. "I'm glad to hear it. Well, I suppose I'll be on my way. I'm so busy these days, what with all those eager beaus coming around." She smiled smugly at Bree.

Her smile faded as Malcolm said, "I'm surprised you entertain beaus if you were so far along with the wedding plans."

Melody sniffed, whirled on her high-laced boot heel and stalked down the sidewalk without a backward glance.

Bree kept her eyes on the tips of her toes. She was embarrassed for Malcolm, but also upset by what Melody said. Was he, in fact, fickle enough to grasp at whatever woman stood in front of him at the time? Would she find herself in Melody's shoes one day soon?

Malcolm's finger under her chin forced her head up. He gazed at her intently. "Bree, my love. Nothing she said is true, except the part about having grown up together. I never entertained marriage to Melody, and she knows it. I've never entertained marriage to anyone, except you. Do you believe me?"

Bree lost herself in his blazing blue eyes. They seemed to pull her toward him, but she realized with a start he was simply finishing what he started before they were interrupted. The kiss was not to be, however.

"Malcolm! I heard you'd returned. Still got the little racecar, eh? You never did take me for that ride you promised," A weathered male voice came from over his shoulder.

With a sigh, Malcolm turned her around to face a white-haired man who leaned heavily on a cane.

Bree watched as Malcolm broke into a broad grin and stepped up to shake the old man's hand. "Caleb, it's good to see you. How have you been?"

"Good 'nuf. Good 'nuf. You tell your mamma I got some mighty fine vegetables coming on. They can start cannin' any time now."

"I'll let her know. We returned yesterday, so it may be a day or two before she's settled and ready to start putting up fruits and vegetables. Caleb, I'd like to introduce you to my fiancée, Bree Barry. We met while I traveled."

Caleb perused her up and down, a toothy smile splitting his face. "She's a beauty, Mal, my boy."

Bree blushed and dipped her head in thanks.

"Well, boy, you born in a barn? Bring her in. Bring her in. Teddy'll want to meet her too, yup, she will."

Malcolm steered Bree inside the building, which turned out to be a store. Bree had never seen, or smelled, anything like it. It seemed to contain everything imaginable. Tall shelves ringed the walls and divided the floor into aisles. Big barrels and wooden crates were scattered in corners and any place there was room to walk by. Fresh produce filled the crates to overflowing, smoked meats and fragrant herbs dangled from the ceiling, bolts of fabric lay willy-nilly on shelves alongside kegs of nails. Her head swam with the effort to see everything. Malcolm urged her forward to a long counter hugging one side of the room. A portly woman stood watching them, her big grin bracketed by fat, rosy cheeks.

She stepped from behind the counter and embraced Malcolm fiercely, but her motherly affection didn't stir a surge of jealousy the way Melody's overly affectionate mauling had. After a few pats on his back, Teddy stepped away and gave him a once-over. "Well, you didn't waste away eatin' all that furin food, so I guess it didn't do you no harm." She looked askance at Bree and back to Malcolm. "Where are your manners, boy?"

He slipped his arm around the woman's beefy shoulder and pushed her over to where Bree stood watching. "Teddy, this is Bree Barry. Bree, this is Theodora Michaels, Caleb's wife. Teddy, Bree and I are going to marry."

"Well I never... What do you think, Caleb? The boy's gettin' married. You tell your ma she can count on me to help. It's been too long without such a joyous occasion. There's still hard feelin's need to be smoothed over, and a wedding's just the thing to do it."

Malcolm agreed and, with a wave, steered Bree out into the bright sunlight. He took a deep breath and grinned at her. "You better get used to it. It's a small town, and we'll be going through this with everyone we meet."

Bree smiled. "I don't mind a bit. I'd like to know all your

friends." She didn't add she hoped that's *all* any of them were, but the thought stuck in the back of her mind. "What are the hard feelings Teddy mentioned?"

"A strike at the mill. People haven't gotten over it yet."

The morning passed quickly. Bree was left with a montage of faces and names swirling in her head, and the fear she'd never get the right name with the right face. They stopped in a small café and lunched on savory lobster cakes and a bottle of light wine. Bree felt quite carefree as they exited the restaurant, but her happiness died as she noticed Eldon leaning casually against the fender of the Mercer.

"Glad you took my advice and decided to tend to your girl, Malcolm. Leaving her on her lonesome while you putter around in an office might put ideas in some young buck's head."

"Don't worry, Eldon. I'll keep Bree close by. In fact, I was just going to take her to the mill for a tour. She and Mother have some splendid ideas for next year's line. I expect they'll both be spending quite of bit of time there with me from now on."

Bree had no trouble figuring out the emotion flickering across Eldon's face this time. It was pure hatred. Malcolm obviously saw it, too. "I'll be calling on the members of the board over the next few weeks. It's time they understand as majority stockholder, I expect to run the company. I'll make sure there's always a place for you, Eldon. Never fear. So long as you and Mother are married, I'll keep you on in some capacity."

"Don't make too many plans, you young pup. I've put a lot of work into the company and the board knows it. They're not going to let you waltz in and take over."

With an enigmatic smile Malcolm replied, "We'll see, won't we?"

Eldon turned on his heel and strode to the Rolls Royce, which idled quietly at the curb. It swerved away into the street with a muted roar, the narrow tires spitting gravel. Bree watched as Malcolm stared after the speeding car with narrowed eyes, his cheek flexing.

* * * *

They spent the afternoon on the promised mill tour. Bree was dumbfounded at the sheer size of the plant. The main building stood two stories tall and covered acres of ground. The weaving shed, boiler building with tall smokestack, cotton and wool warehouses and cottages for the workers spread out even more. Inside the factory, she held her hands over her ears to shut out the din as hundreds of bobbins fed white threads into clattering weaving machines nonstop. Malcolm showed her other rooms used for carding, looping, knitting and warping, explaining how different parts of the mill turned out nubby woolens, smooth worsteds, cambric, satin, lawn, batiste, linen and silks. Once woven, the plain fabrics would be sent to finishing factories for bleaching and dyeing before going on to their last stop to be made into garments. He promised to show her those factories soon.

Bree was a bit fatigued when they returned to the house and Malcolm insisted she take a nap before dinner. She awoke refreshed and quickly dressed in a light frock. After she brushed out her hair, she secured it with a matching ribbon and allowed it to tumble down her back to please Malcolm. Anxious to see him again, she bounced merrily down the stairs but came to a halt when she heard voices from below.

She stopped on the landing and peered over the railing. Eldon leaned casually against the jamb in the parlor doorway, talking to someone inside. Bree couldn't make out the muted voice. She walked more sedately down the remaining steps. Eldon caught her movement and turned to face her, a smug expression settling on his face.

"Ah, and here she is. The lovely Bree. Come in, my dear. We were having a drink before dinner."

Bree entered the room, searching for Malcolm. Instead, she spied Melody draped languorously across the settee, a dainty stemmed glass dangling from her hand. Bree stumbled to a stop and looked around, but Elizabeth and Malcolm were not in the room.

Melody raised her glass in a casual salute. "Good evening, Miss Barry. I hope you don't mind. Eldon invited me to join you for dinner. It seems so natural to be here. I've probably spent as much time in this house as my own, ever since I was a child. If you have any questions about the family, or Malcolm, please feel free to ask. I'm sure I can enlighten you." With a coy smile partially hidden behind her hand, she continued, "Of course, there are some questions I won't answer. I mean, they're just too personal to get into. I'm sure you understand." The blonde smiled dreamily.

Bree understood, all right. "Why, Melody, you have no idea how much fun I'm having getting to know all about Malcolm on my own. As for Elizabeth, the two of use share a rare bond. After all, we survived the *Titanic* sinking." Bree bit the inside of her cheek to keep from smiling as she saw Melody's eyes narrow and her smirk dim.

Voices echoed from the hall and Malcolm and Elizabeth entered. Malcolm's gaze fastened on Bree's, and he smiled as he strode to her, ignoring the other two occupants.

He was only a step away when Melody called out, "Malcolm, we've been waiting for you. Dear Bree is trying her best to be a hostess, but I don't think she's had much experience at it. I'm sure it's hard to suddenly be thrown into a life so different from anything she's known." She simpered. "Eldon explained about your dear Bree's background."

Instead of acknowledging Melody or Eldon, Malcolm continued to Bree's side where he greeted her with a peck on the cheek. He pulled her under the protection of his arm and, as she looked deep into his eyes, gave her a reassuring smile.

Malcolm turned to face Melody. "Perhaps Eldon didn't explain *everything* about Bree's background. Did he tell you she spent most of her life in a castle as a close confidante to an English peer of the realm? I'm sure our much more modest home is nothing special to her. It might be she's more used to having visitors announce their intentions in advance, but she'll soon settle in to our more casual way of life."

Bree was surprised, and grateful. With a few words he'd given Melody the impression she had been a friend of the Rothberrys, rather than a servant, and handed out a subtle rebuke for the woman's arriving unannounced.

Eldon directed his comments to his wife. "I didn't think you'd mind if I invited Melody to dinner, Elizabeth. She's such a close family friend. It appears Malcolm has forgotten."

Bree saw Elizabeth's eyes flick back and forth between her husband and son, her indecision clear. She said, "It's wonderful to meet your childhood friends, Malcolm. I hope I'll have the opportunity often. I certainly don't want any changes made to your usual habits because I'm here."

Bree heard Malcolm's low snort of amusement at her wording, which relegated Melody to a playmate rather than a lover.

Elizabeth smiled at Bree gratefully then spoke to her son, "Malcolm, perhaps you'd get Bree and me a bit of wine?"

The next few minutes were filled with awkward silence as Malcolm busied himself with the drinks. A collective sigh of relief sounded when the maid stepped in and announced dinner.

In the large formal dining room, Eldon and Elizabeth occupied the head and foot of the table, with Malcolm and Bree on one side and Melody by herself on the other. The blonde seemed incapable of taking her amber eyes off Malcolm. Bree was relieved he didn't seem to care, directing most of his comments to herself or his mother. She noticed Eldon watching Malcolm, a hard glint in his eyes. When the elder DuMont noticed Bree's gaze, he quickly replaced the sneer with a look of polite interest.

At Malcolm's prompting, Melody explained she'd run into Eldon while in town and when he invited her to dinner, couldn't wait to see Elizabeth and hear all about their trip to the Continent. Elizabeth seemed a bit perplexed at Melody's gushing enthusiasm, but obliged with details about their time in France.

"And what about when the *Titanic* sank? The papers said hundreds of people drowned. Did you know any of them? Did you see them? It must have been horrible." Melody's eyes were bright with prying curiosity and she pressed Elizabeth for details until the older woman kindly, but firmly, told her the memories were too painful to discuss.

Bree was confused at Eldon's manner during dinner. He seemed to take every opportunity to bring up how close Malcolm and Melody were and how much they had in common, while emphasizing how little his stepson knew about his fiancée. It seemed to her Eldon subtly hinted Malcolm might simply be bewitched with her for the moment, and what he felt was only gratitude for saving his mother. Malcolm and Elizabeth didn't seem to notice, and Bree chastised herself for reading more into Eldon's words than what was really there, but felt exhausted and depressed by the time the table was cleared. When Elizabeth suggested everyone make an early night of it and steered Melody to the door a short time later, she mentally cheered.

Chapter 26

Bree woke later than usual the next morning, disoriented from a nightmare. She shook her head to clear it from the vision of her brothers and father smiling down at her over the gunwale of a lifeboat as she sank under the dark waters. She climbed out of bed, missed the step stool and landed in a painful heap. Tears threatened and, in her depressed mood, required unusual effort to quell.

Pulling on her wrapper, she walked over to the window and pushed back the curtain, hoping to be soothed by the beautiful garden. But then she saw two figures walking close together.

Malcolm and Melody. The blonde's arm looped in his and she leaned into his shoulder. He stared down into her upturned face.

An icicle of cold fear hardened in Bree's chest. Melody was beautiful, she and Malcolm had grown up together, and she obviously wanted him for herself. Their families were close. In contrast, Malcolm had only met Bree a few scant weeks ago and they really had little in common--she came from poor people and a messy family life. He was rich, had a loving mother, and a business to run. Did he already regret his decision to marry her? He had defended her, and was still tender and loving. But would it last?

Her musings only sucked her deeper into despondency. She jerked on the first dress she touched in the closet. Instead of leaving her hair loose, she wrenched it back into a simple braid, giving up battling tendrils that kept escaping around her face. The small dining room was empty when she wandered in, and she picked at eggs and maple-cured bacon heaped on her plate by a solicitous maid. Malcolm was conspicuously absent. Were he and Melody still in the garden?

Realizing her second cup of tea had gone cold, she went to the parlor and looked out the window. Seeing no sign of the pair, she found the latch and opened the big door. She hurried down the wide flight of shallow steps to the path, and swiftly walked through the gardens. Her feet moved faster and faster, neck craning to see over the carefully tended topiaries. But they weren't there. Feeling alone in the world, she turned her steps over to the oversize stone barn, seeking solace in its dark corners. As she drew near, she heard voices.

Just inside the big sliding doors she came upon Malcolm and an older man standing with a horse. The mare turned her head at Bree's approach, drawing the men's attention.

Malcolm smiled and walked toward her. "There you are, sleepy head. I was beginning to wonder if I should check on you."

Bree forced a smile. Would he mention his early morning tryst with Melody? She couldn't bring herself to ask, fearing his answer.

"I want you to meet Murray. He's the head stable boy."

Bree thought it odd to call the old man a stable boy, but her mind was still wrapped around Malcolm and Melody and what they were talking about earlier. She nodded absently in his direction. He touched his cap and gave a bob of a bow.

"I've never asked. Can you ride?" Malcolm questioned.

"A little. We had a pony, but I didn't have much opportunity to ride." *Another thing we don't know about each other.*

"We've several gentle horses here. We'll have you riding like the wind in no time, won't we, Murray?" Malcolm smiled and the old man nodded emphatically.

Bree tried to get excited at the prospect, but knew she hadn't been successful when Malcolm queried, "Are you feeling all right, dear? You seem downcast."

"Just a bad dream." Bree shivered at the thought her wonderful new life could yet turn into a horrible nightmare. If Malcolm put her aside and set her adrift in the new country, what would become of her?

Malcolm stepped close and pulled her into his embrace. "It's chilly. You should have a wrap, or better yet, let's find Mother. She made me promise we'd go to the factory and start looking at ideas for the new line today. And she especially wanted you to be there. With you two talented women, the DuMont dresses will be the talk of the town come next season." He gave her a squeeze and turned her toward the house.

Bree smiled up at him, but inside, her heart seemed to stutter. Not a word had been spoken about what Melody and he were doing together earlier.

Chapter 27

Fred Dunby turned away, his red hair hidden under the broad-brimmed derby hat. He reeled from the shock of seeing the man from the *Titanic* lifeboat sitting right there in the car as it passed. Luckily, DuMont had been focused on something in his lap and hadn't noticed Fred standing on the curb. The car stopped a block away. The big man exited and hurried down the alley as the car accelerated and disappeared around the corner. Fred set off after him, keeping a healthy distance.

He wasn't sure what good it would do to follow DuMont, but he figured the more he knew about the lying sneak, the better chance he'd eventually get what he deserved. The New York police had threatened to lock Fred up when he tried to tell them what really happened in the lifeboat. They might not have believed a lowly sailor, but they had passed his story on to the shipping line and he'd heard from some friends White Star was searching for him. If they got a hold of him, he'd likely face charges--bad ones--for stealing the lifeboat, and maybe murder if he couldn't convince some of his shipmates to come forward with the whole story.

Fred couldn't sleep anymore. Visions of Chief Steward Latimer's surprised expression as he slumped to the deck, his head with a neat little hole in it bouncing off the railings with a metallic clang, haunted him. The cries of children calling for their mothers, the thrashing of drowning passengers echoed in his ears, all while his own lifeboat bobbed safely along, nearly empty. He'd accept any punishment, so long as Mr. High-and-Mighty DuMont got his as well. It wasn't right the man got off Scott-free just because he was a nob.

Fred followed the dark suit, stepping carefully so as not to alert his quarry. Eldon turned and sauntered up a few steps to a back stoop before knocking three times, then twice more, then a final time on the door of a big three-story house. It opened and he slipped inside. Fred couldn't see anything but shadows through the heavily curtained windows, but it seemed several people moved about. He looked around and found a corner behind some ash cans to hunker down and wait.

Once, a pretty young woman wearing naught but a silk wrapper came out the door with a box of trash. She walked toward him and he flattened himself in dust, and worse, as she deposited the trash in a dustbin. A short while later another man was admitted after he used the coded knock, then a different man came out. Fred thought about it, and decided the building was either a gambling hall or a whorehouse. Either way, if he played his cards right, he would find a way to make life miserable for the bastard.

The second schooner of beer he'd had for lunch was making him mighty uncomfortable an hour later when DuMont reappeared and headed back to the street where the fancy car waited.

Once it motored out of sight, Fred ambled out of the alley and sat on the stoop of an empty storefront, pondering his next step. He didn't need to follow the car. He'd already visited the rich estate where the man lived. It had cost him a pretty penny to get on the train in New York, but he hadn't wanted to risk never finding the man again after seeing him in the station. After watching DuMont's party disembark in the hamlet of Linton, he made a beeline for the local pub. It only took a few beers and friendly conversation with the locals to find out who the man was and where he lived. It took him the better part of a day to walk to the house and back, after spending time scouting around for good places to spy on the occupants.

Fred made a mental note to find out exactly what went on in the house off the alley then slouched back to the dingy boarding house where he had a room. He would take his time and do this right. He wasn't likely to get another chance.

Chapter 28

Melody tried on yet another dress, stepping over the pile of discarded gowns already on the floor. She knew Marybeth would be livid when she had to re-iron them, but she didn't care. All that mattered was when the post arrived earlier it included a note inviting the Parsons family to a community get-together at the DuMont home so everyone could meet Bree Barry. It was important Melody make a good impression at the soiree. She had to convince Malcolm he'd chosen the wrong woman, or at least manage to drive the girl off.

Her mother burst into the room, a haze of flowery perfume trailing behind. She waded right through the pile of clothing and plopped down on the bed. "What do you intend to do about Malcolm now, my dear?" she demanded without preamble.

Melody gritted her teeth. How like her mother to expect her to come up with all the ideas. Between them, her parents didn't seem to have a clue how to keep the family fortune together. "Why, I'm going to show Malcolm he's made a big mistake, and convince him I'm willing to overlook his foolishness this one time. But he'll pay for it before I'm done."

"You'd *better* convince him. If something doesn't happen soon, we'll lose the mill, our home, and everything we own. I do not intend to go to the poor house because you weren't able to hold on to your man," her mother griped.

Melody whirled in fury. "If Father had any business sense at all we wouldn't be in this mess!"

Her mother didn't flinch. "If your father had any business sense, he would have sold the damn mill to Percy when he offered to buy it. But no, he played coy and demanded more money. Even then, Percy probably would have paid it if he hadn't up and died on us." She stood and paced, then stopped in front of Melody. She grasped her daughter's chin in a hard grip and tilted her head side to side. "There's not a prettier girl in the whole state. If it was just beauty Malcolm craved, we wouldn't have a worry in the world." She paused, frowning. "Although I heard this Bree is lovely." She glanced at her daughter, seeking confirmation.

"Hah! Who did you hear that from? She's no better than a child, with pasty skin, hideous red hair and *freckles* for God's sake." Even as she played down Bree's appearance, Melody knew she was quite extraordinary. Malcolm's fiancée might look young, but the body under the stylish clothes was that of a full-grown woman. Melody turned back to the mirror and closely observed her own figure. She was taller, more *statuesque*, she thought with a smile, then frowned as she noted her breasts were not quite as prominent as the redhead's. If Mother was any indication, her hips would eventually broaden too much but until then Melody felt confident she could outshine that country bumpkin Bridget if given the proper presentation.

She kicked at the pile of rumpled clothing. "I need a new gown for the party."

"And how do you expect to pay for it?" her mother snapped. "We've no credit left in town."

"You'll have to find it. I can't attend the party in any of these-- everyone has seen them before."

Her mother got a sly gleam in her eye. "Perhaps if we hurry we can get Mrs. Belvins to make you a dress on Malcolm's credit before she finds out he has a fiancée. She's so hard of hearing, unless someone has told her straight out, she won't know a thing." She stood and bustled out of the room.

Melody sighed with relief. If Mother was good at anything, it was wringing concessions out of the trade's people. If anyone could finagle a new dress, her mother could. It might be the last unless she won Malcolm over. She sat at the dressing table and played with her hair to find a becoming style for the party.

Chapter 29

Elizabeth and Bree flipped through the design book. The older woman mourned the loss of her sketches from her recent trip to France, but at Bree's and Malcolm's urging had been trying to recreate what she could remember.

Malcolm sat at the desk in his office at the mill, watching the two women so intently discussing fashion details. Their faces were close together--one mature, the other young--one with pale hair, the other with masses of deep auburn. His heart gave a hard thump as he thought how close he'd come to losing them both. He couldn't imagine life without either of them.

He had thought, under the circumstances, his mother would allow a quick wedding but that hope had been kyboshed immediately. Elizabeth adamantly insisted on sufficient time to put together the wedding she always envisioned for her only son. He was slightly pacified by the engagement party that was in the works. The entire county had been invited to meet Bree. Malcolm knew such a large party would be a burden for the house staff so soon after the family's return, but he was anxious to let everyone know he'd found his one true love.

Malcolm's thoughts turned to Melody and her accusations. Maybe he *had* expected he would marry Melody eventually. It would have been a huge mistake. Marriage to someone as demanding and selfish as her would have been painfully uncomfortable, in addition to saddling him with her harridan of a mother and a drunken sot for a father-in-law. Parsons had financial problems, made worse when Eldon refused to do business with the mill. That was something Malcolm intended to change--not for Melody or her greedy family, but for the workers Parsons employed.

* * * *

Bree raised her head and saw Malcolm watching them intently. She smiled timidly and received a grin in return. Her heart leapt. He *must* care for her. He couldn't possibly look at her with such love if he intended to send her away. He seemed impatient to wed her and excited about the party. She wished Melody weren't invited, but the annoying woman stopped by and accepted the invitation in person, cooing about the dress she intended to wear. She even had the nerve to say she expected Malcolm to inspect every inch of it and tell her how it compared to the current French fashions. The dark-blue frock Melody had worn that morning, and which she referred to as "this old thing," set off her fair hair to perfection, and the low-cut bodice exposed far too much creamy bosom to Bree's thinking. If the new gown was anywhere near as lovely as she bragged, every man's eyes would be on the blonde, maybe even Malcolm's.

Elizabeth interrupted her morose thoughts. "Oh, Bree, dear, this one would be perfect for you."

Bree forced her mind off Melody and back to the book. Elizabeth pointed at a beautiful gown. "The style is exactly right. We'll do your hair up high." The older woman grew more excited as she added details with a pencil. "We'll add a rosette here and extend the lace so it drapes over your wrists. She turned to her son. "Malcolm, we still have several yards of that heavy caramel satin from our test run, don't we?"

"I believe so. I'll run check. When I return, we'd best get back home. Bertie will have dinner on the table and no one to eat it." He left the room.

By the time he returned, Elizabeth had made several more alterations to the design, and Bree shook her head in wonder. "I never would have thought to add those tassels. I'm sure you're as good a designer as any of the French."

Elizabeth blushed and shook her head, but Bree could see she was pleased.

* * * *

The night before the event Elizabeth retired early, exhausted from endless preparations over the past few weeks. Bree stayed up, working frantically to put the finishing touches on her party dress. Elizabeth's gown, completed earlier in the day, hung in the corner. Malcolm hadn't yet returned from a late day at one of the finishing mills. He'd been busy the whole week trying to refamiliarize himself with the company's myriad operations.

188

It was late when she laid her finished gown on the cutting table and wandered down to the parlor. The nights were still cool as summer made a tardy appearance and a small fire burned in the grate, making the room cozy and casting flickering shadows on the walls. She drew near and stared into the flames, mesmerized by the dancing colors. The front door opened and she heard footsteps crossing the floor. With a happy smile, she turned and took several steps before she realized it was Eldon who stood before her.

A slow smile crept over his face, and shivers of revulsion ran down her back. As he advanced, Bree retreated until she felt the heat of the fire. She glanced back and realized flames licked only inches from her skirt. She took an involuntary step forward and found herself pressed to Eldon's chest. His arms slithered around her back and pulled her tight.

"My, my, what an enjoyable welcome, dear Bree. Had I known you were here waiting for me with such eagerness, I would have hurried."

She struggled in his embrace, but his arms tightened painfully, causing her to gasp for breath. "Let me go, Mr. DuMont." She couldn't bear to call him by his given name. "I thought you were Malcolm. I want to go to my room now."

He chuckled deep in his throat and shook his head, eyes hooded. He leaned down, his mouth so close to her ear she could feel the warmth of his breath, and goose bumps rose on her skin. "I'd like to go to your room too, my dear. We could have a bit of fun while I taught you so many things. Why, by the time we finished, you'd know exactly how to please Malcolm. I could correct your mistakes and save him ever so much time."

Wincing in disgust, Bree turned away. Eldon let go with one hand and his long fingers fastened on her chin, inexorably turning her face toward him. Horrified, she saw his head lower. He intended to kiss her! She struggled harder, her heart racing. "Let me be. Stop it!"

"Yes, Eldon. Do stop," Malcolm commanded from across the room.

Bree stumbled back as Eldon shoved her away and whirled to face his stepson. Malcolm strode toward them, fists bunched, and swung at Eldon. Bree screamed at a sudden searing pain.

Chapter 30

When Eldon shoved her, Bree stepped back toward the fire. The hem of her dress landed in the coals and smoldered only an instant before igniting. The underskirts burst into flame and the entire back was alight almost immediately.

Malcolm swerved from his direct path toward Eldon. He caught her arm, pushing Bree to the floor, and rolled her across the carpet while trying to strip off his jacket with one hand. As soon as the jacket came free, he wrapped it around her lower body and smothered the flames. Eldon fled the room. In an effort to make sure the gown no longer smoldered, Malcolm tore at the shredded fabric of her skirt and slips and in a moment, she was naked from the waist down. Bree gasped in pain and plucked at her calves. He realized her silk stockings were melted onto her skin.

The sound of running feet caused Malcolm to drape his jacket over Bree's exposed limbs and he moved around to shield her from the doorway. Hannah, the maid, stopped as she saw Malcolm kneeling over a prostrate Bree.

191

"I thought I heard a scream, sir." The maid's forehead crinkled and her mouth widened into an "O" as she looked back and forth between Malcolm and Bree. He knew how it must appear, with Bree flat on her back, clothing scattered around the room, and him hovering over her.

"Fetch my mother. Miss Bridget's been burned. And get her a wrapper."

The maid's eyes widened. "Yes, sir." She turned on her heel and fled.

Elizabeth, wrapped in a robe, her hair covered with a frilly satin cap, rushed in a few moments later. She examined Bree's legs closely then sent Hannah for fresh butter when the maid returned with Bree's robe.

"I don't think it burned too deeply. The butter will soften the skin and help get the stockings off." She looked into Bree's tear-filled eyes. "It will be painful for a while, but I don't think there will be any scarring."

Bree bit her lip and squirmed as the stockings were peeled off, but as Elizabeth said, the burns were mostly superficial. Malcolm left for several moments and returned with a small crock of ointment, which he rubbed over the reddened areas.

"This is a special concoction old Murray makes. It's a recipe his family has handed down for generations. I don't know what's in it, but it will heal almost anything. It seems to help a great deal with pain as well. He's used it on all of us at one time or another, and on most of the animals around here too." He grinned at the expression of distaste on her face. "I think he keeps the stuff for the animals in a different jar," he said, trying to tease away her fear.

Bree smiled then yawned.

Elizabeth stood and pointed at the stairs. "To bed with you both. Tomorrow is a busy day, and I want Bree to get plenty of rest. She may not feel like dancing tomorrow, but I think she'll still enjoy the party." She helped the maid gather the scorched fabric scraps then headed upstairs.

Malcolm helped Bree to her feet. "I'd carry you, but I'm afraid I'd hurt your legs more than if you walk."

"I'm fine. It doesn't hurt at all now. That salve is amazing."

The tie on her robe slipped loose and the soft fabric gaped open, drawing Malcolm's attention to the exposed silken thighs, the tiny area of auburn fluff standing out against her pale skin. He swallowed a hard lump that suddenly stuck in his throat and forced his eyes back to her face.

Bree gasped, jerking the robe close and hurriedly retying the belt. She stared at him, a deep rose suffusing her face. Her eyes widened at his expression.

Malcolm knew he probably resembled a wolf contemplating a rabbit. The instinct to pull her to him, raining kisses over her body as his hands sought out the now-hidden treasure, was strong. Only the trusting look in her beautiful green eyes stayed him.

He gave her a lopsided grin. "The benefits of marriage are becoming more and more obvious," he quipped, unrepentant.

* * * *

Bree couldn't quite suppress a grin as his risqué comment. She took his offered hand and allowed him to lead her up to her room. He pushed the door open with his shoulder and kicked it closed behind as he enfolded her within his arms, continuing inexorably toward the bed. As they bumped against the bedrail, she glanced up at him, hesitant.

Malcolm gazed down at her, searching her face. She couldn't draw away from his hypnotic eyes as they seemed to take over her will. His head swooped down and captured her lips. He crushed her soft breasts against his rock-hard chest. The suddenness of his embrace shocked her, its intensity urging her arms up to slip around his neck. Passion burned from her very core. Except for their one memorable encounter on the train, his kisses had always been somewhat chaste, leaving her hungry for more, ashamed of her wantonness. His hands rubbed her back, lower and lower until they grasped her buttocks and drew her close. She felt his hardness throbbing against her belly. Bree was torn between knowing she should pull away before it was too late, and the intense desire to see what would happen next.

In a fluid movement, Malcolm turned and they fell together on the bed. Bree gasped in surprise as he rolled, pulling her full length on top of him.

His mouth hovered beneath her pleasantly bruised lips. "Bree, my love. Waiting is killing me. Let me take you. Let me show you how I love you," he whispered hoarsely.

She nestled closer in answer, wriggling her knee between his thighs as she bent down and returned his kiss twofold. He moaned against her lips as his hands slid to her shoulders and pushed the robe away. It caught, and he slipped his hands between their bodies, fumbling with the tie. She held herself up with outstretched arms, hands on either side of his head. The remnants of her gown were tossed away. She felt cool air on her backside, but her body was afire with a compelling, unknown need. He bent a knee and his thigh pressed against her exposed, sensitive mound, rubbing lightly.

Dusky moonlight illuminated the room. As his gleaming gaze roved over the planes and curves and shadowy nooks of her body, heat rushed to her face. Even hotter was the juncture of her legs where his muscular thigh caused ripples of something she'd never felt before. His mouth closed over a breast, and she shivered as he gently suckled. His long, strong fingers gently squeezed and played with its mate. Sighing, she arched her back in ecstasy. His other hand busily roamed down the deep indent of her spine, over her rounded buttocks and deeper.

He touched her core, first tentatively, gently, then stroking the lips of her femininity harder, teasing her with flicks of his fingers against the moist folds. Her head snapped forward and she gasped.

"Don't fear me, love. I will never hurt you. Let me," he whispered, his breath hot on the sensitive skin of her breast. His tongue licked and played at the tight nipple and she felt she might swoon. Bree gripped his shoulders as a long, strong finger began to explore the depths of her womanhood, teasing and tantalizing, deeper. His tongue skated away from the hard tip of her breast, as he lapped kisses across her collarbone and up her neck. His mouth came to rest on hers, where the velvet softness of his tongue slipped past the seam of her mouth and set off a whole new wave of sensations. So many feelings surged through her body. Bree struggled to focus, but his hand was doing things, wonderful things, and his tongue continued to seek out the recesses of her mouth. She could taste him, smell him, feel him, inside and all around her.

Unable to control her desire, Bree struggled to free the buttons of his shirt. As they pulled loose, she impatiently brushed the fabric aside. Her fingers caressed the firm expanse of his chest, her nail grazing his nipple and sending a shiver through him. Down over the washboard hardness of his stomach her restless, curious hands trailed, following the line of fine hair to the waist of his trousers.

With another quick roll, she found herself on her back as Malcolm loomed over her. "Finish it," he begged. She undid the fastenings of his trousers and shoving them down as he wriggled to help. Then suddenly he was there, hot and hard. She felt his manhood pulsing against her hip. His hands were relentless on her body, touching, caressing, tempting. *Oh, God! This is exquisite torture.*

"I want you now, my sweet. But I won't force you. Will you have me?" Malcolm murmured.

"Yes." The word would have been a scream, if he hadn't smothered it with a kiss. Her nails raked his shoulders; her hands straining to pull him close as her body commanded more. *More.*

His hand slipped under her and shifted her hips. His knee, already sending her into paroxysms as it continued to rub along the sensitive mound, pushed her thighs apart. He drew back a fraction and stared deep into her eyes. She nodded encouragement. She felt him probe, the velvety softness pushing, entering. She bucked against him at the fleeting moment of pain. Then the sting was only a vague memory. Excitement--no, something much, much more--grew as he slowly thrust deeper. He filled her and a sense of greedy anticipation grew. She couldn't stop now, wouldn't let him stop. She had to know where he was taking her. Needed to know what she would find there. Malcolm moved inside her slowly. An overwhelming sense of wanting more--more of him, more of the intoxicating feelings he stirred, enveloped her. She clutched at him, lunging to meet his thrusts. Words of love and surrender tumbled from Bree's lips as she buried her face in his neck.

His pace increased. Malcolm's breath came harsh and quick. She pulled back, watching him. His eyes were closed and an expression of exultation lit his features. Bree felt a new spark deep within her. It burst into flames and scorched her soul with a sudden fiery explosion, threatening to consume her. "Malcolm!" The sudden sensation brought tears to her eyes. A sob rose, as she tried to comprehend the incredible feeling that emerged from where he joined with her. The sensation washed over her, leaving her sensitive to each inch of his skin touching hers. She wondered if they had somehow melted together, like the silk of her stockings to her legs. With a final thrust, he groaned and collapsed on top of her, his mouth finding her neck and giving her nibbling kisses as his arms clasped her tightly. Malcolm rolled to his side and pulled her with him.

Sated, they lay together for a long time. Her fingertips lightly brushed across his back and arms and her lips skimmed his chest. He nuzzled her temple, while one hand played with the mass of curls wrapped around his arm.

"I want to stay here forever," he murmured.

Bree smiled. She knew she should be ashamed, but this felt so right. "I'm afraid it might cause a bit of excitement in the morning when Hannah comes in to stoke the fire."

"You wouldn't need a fire if I were with you."

Bree laughed softly. It was true; she basked in his warm, radiant heat.

The moon had passed behind the trees when, with a loud sigh, he raised himself from her side. "I'm going, but not for long. You and Mother better get this wedding thing settled quickly, or Hannah will have to learn to live with finding me in your bed, or you in mine." Malcolm bent down and gave her another deep kiss. As she slipped her arms around his neck and drew him down, he shook his head. "Stop that, you little wanton. I've given you a taste of what you can expect as my wife. That's going to have to be enough for now. I don't have the willpower to leave if we get started again." He slapped her lightly on the derriere and bent to gather his clothing.

Bree stretched like a cat. His scent lingered on her skin--the mix of spice and soap and man. She rolled onto her stomach and kicked her feet playfully as she watched him pull on his trousers.

"My God. You look like you're ten years old right now, but a few minutes ago you were all woman." Malcolm stared at her a moment

198

before shaking his head.

He bent and kissed her on the forehead, then turned and hurried out the room, closing the door gently.

"Good night," she called. Once she donned a long flannel nightgown, she snuggled into the downy mattress. She hugged herself, closing her eyes as she conjured memories of the last hour.

Chapter 31

Malcolm leaned against his door, taking deep breaths. He fought the urge to return to Bree's room. He was amazed to find his ardor already quickening again. Seeking a distraction, he stepped to the side table holding a rarely used decanter of whiskey. He sloshed a few fingers of the amber liquid into a stubby glass and took a big sip. Eyes closed, he savored the oaky burn. A smile washed his face as he recalled Bree's responses to his lovemaking. He was just now beginning to realize how enjoyable marriage to the fiery Irishwoman would to be. He would have her in his bed every night, and didn't intend to let her out of his sight for much of the day, either.

He walked to the window and glanced out. Across the garden, he saw the windows of the manor's master suite. A light shone in his mother's bedroom, but Eldon's windows were dark. Malcolm's face hardened as the memory of what Eldon had been doing as he came upon the pair in the parlor. When he'd rounded the doorway to find his fiancée in his stepfather's embrace, he'd been momentarily shocked. But he immediately became aware Bree struggled to break free and heard her protests. A massive surge of anger toward Eldon filled him again. If not for the fire, he had no doubt a violent altercation would have ensued. The next time they met, Eldon would have reason to seriously regret trespassing on Malcolm's domain.

* * * *

In his darkened room at the other side of the house, Eldon's thoughts were also focused on Bree. He too stood at the window, peering though slitted drapes. He watched as the girl's room went dark. Ever since he'd had Bree in his arms, Eldon hadn't been able to get her out of his mind. He still felt her firm breasts against his chest. His hands ached to squeeze them, and his groin throbbed with the desire to plumb the depths of her delicious young body.

Eldon recalled the surge of excitement that filled him as Malcolm came into the room. His hand had immediately reached into his pocket for the pistol he now carried with him all the time. A vision of a dead Malcolm on the floor next to him as he had his way with Bree almost made him dizzy. If the girl hadn't screamed and distracted Malcolm, he knew he would have acted. And, while it would have been satisfying to kill his stepson, the satisfaction would have been short-lived. He needed a plan that left Malcolm dead and didn't land him in jail. Confident he could come up with something, Eldon decided to relieve the pressure in his trousers before he focused on Malcolm's demise. He took the back stairs down to the stable and started his recently purchased Pierce Arrow, preferring to drive himself so as not to pique Carlisle's curiosity. In town, he pulled the dust-covered car into the alley and parked behind a screening hedge.

Even at the late hour, the door opened immediately to his coded knock. The madam greeted him with a smile.

He demanded, "I trust you followed my instructions?"

She nodded. "I have a girl I think will suit you. As you specified, she has red hair and is, as yet, unsoiled. I do not deal in underage girls, but as she only recently reached her majority, I think you will find she meets your requirements. She's upstairs in room number three. If you'll give me a moment, I'll wake her."

"No need." Eldon took the stairs two at a time, ripping off his jacket and jerking open his shirt as he went.

* * * *

Nearly an hour later he sauntered down the steps, pulling his jacket on. He frowned as he realized several of the buttons on his shirt were missing--a result of his earlier eagerness.

The madam stood at the bottom of the stairs, her expression anxious. Perhaps he should have done a better job muffling the girl's cries. Mrs. Zubrinsky bit her lip. "There will, of course, be additional costs for tonight."

He paused then took the last two steps, stopping inches from her face. She retreated a few feet until she fetched up against the wall. He followed, bending in close. "I will pay a fair price, as always. Don't press your luck, my dear. You wouldn't want the neighbors to know what goes on in your so-called 'Home for Unwed Mothers,' now would you?"

She swallowed hard and crossed her arms. Then, with more spunk than he expected, she raised her chin and snapped, "No more than your family would want to know what you do here, *Mr. Smith.*"

"I think we understand each other," he gritted and turned to the door. As he left, Eldon pondered whether the woman would be a problem. He shook his head. If things went like they should, he wouldn't have to reside in this backwoods town for much longer, and he'd have no further use for her services.

Chapter 32

The day of the party dawned bright and sunny, just like Bree's mood. She broke into an Irish ditty as she enjoyed a bath. Her gaze repeatedly drifted to the big bed, framed in the doorway, as she replayed memories of last night. Soon she and Malcolm would lie together every night.

Bree met Hannah on the stairs as she skipped down to breakfast. The maid inquired about her injuries, and Bree was surprised to realize she felt no pain at all and, in fact, the fire had been pushed out of her mind by thoughts of Malcolm.

Being reminded about what happened with Eldon the night before sobered Bree, and she walked sedately into the dining room to find Elizabeth and Malcolm already seated. He turned and smiled, rising to help her into her chair. As she bent to arrange her napkin, he pressed a kiss at the side of her neck, giving her shoulders a squeeze.

"How are you feeling, my love?"

Bree flashed a delighted smile at the endearment. "I'm fine. I don't know what's in that salve, but Mr. Murray could be a rich man if he sold it."

Malcolm laughed. "He'll never give up the secret." He sat next to her and glanced back and forth between the two women. "I know today is going to be busy. What can I do to help?"

Elizabeth observed them with a gentle smile. "You can stay out of the way, my boy. The staff knows what needs done. Why don't you go fishing or take a drive in that silly car of yours? Just be sure to return in time to change for the party."

He made a wry face. "I can see I'm not wanted."

"That's not true. I want you." The words were out of Bree's mouth before she realized what she'd said.

Malcolm and Elizabeth both laughed. "I'm glad to hear it," he said with a knowing smile, squeezing Bree's hand under the table as she blushed furiously.

As soon as breakfast was finished, Malcolm dutifully headed out, and the two women turned themselves to the final tasks before the party.

* * * *

Eldon watched Malcolm roar off in the Mercer, a haze of dust hovering in his wake. He'd returned to the house in the wee hours of the morning, and quietly made his way to his room for a change of clothing. It seemed prudent to make himself scarce for the day, but with Malcolm gone now there was no need to put himself out.

He ambled out to the barn and waited for Murray to saddle his favorite gelding. He stared at the chaff floating in the sunlight and brooded over the multitude of arrangements he needed to set into motion. Too bad the board of directors couldn't observe his organizational skills today--they'd be quite impressed. Just another example of why he was so much better suited to running the company than his wife's whelp. Yes, indeed, there was quite a lot to do before the festivities began. Eldon mentally rubbed his hands in glee.

Just as he started to take Murray to task for his slowness, the groom led the horse over and offered a leg up. Snorting, Eldon threw himself in the saddle and jerked the gelding around, forcing the horse's broad chest to catch the groom in the shoulder and knock him to the ground.

Without a backward glance, he rode down a nearby trail toward the village. He left his mount at the livery at the far end of town. There were more and more motorcars in the area, but many of the old-timers insisted on keeping their horses and carriages on the roads. And today Eldon wanted to attract as little attention as possible. There was no telling when or where Malcolm might turn up, and the Rolls and Pierce Arrow were far too well known to escape the younger man's attention. With his hat pulled low over his brow, he set out down a pretty residential lane. The houses here were large and well cared for, with lush lawns, wrought iron or freshly painted picket fences, mature trees and large flower gardens ringing the structures. He lifted the latch on the gate of a handsome two-story manor and took the blue-gray slate steps two at a time. He rang the bell. A uniformed maid opened the door quickly and, recognizing Eldon, led him into the immaculate parlor to await her mistress.

Melody rushed into the room a few moments later, her flushed, animated face falling when she saw him.

"Why, my dear. You don't seem pleased to see me. Or is it that you expected Malcolm would be your gentleman caller?" Eldon asked with a sardonic drawl.

Melody shrugged a shoulder daintily. "I'm surprised to see you is all, Eldon. What is so important it brings you to town? I'll be at the house this evening, you know."

Eldon paused and reviewed the speech he'd perfected on the ride in. "You'd better sit down, dear. What I have to say may come as a shock. A welcome one, I think," he added as her eyes widened.

Melody collapsed into a thickly upholstered chair. "What is it? Is Malcolm all right? What has that red-headed minx done now?"

Eldon laughed. "And why would you think Bree has anything to do with why I'm here?" Seeing anger and concern battling in her eyes, he relented. "Malcolm is fine. In fact, I think he's finally coming to his senses." He held her full attention now. "I overheard Malcolm speaking with Elizabeth. Yes, I know, eavesdropping is a nasty habit, but in this case I think you'll be happy I lingered." Eldon enjoyed keeping her in suspense.

"What did he say?" Melody scooted to the edge of her seat.

"It seems the spell of dear Bree's beauty is beginning to wear off. Malcolm is tiring of the girl. I don't think he realized how young and inexperienced she is. I expect it feels rather like taking a friend's younger sister on a date. She also started making demands for new clothes and wants to bring her entire family from Ireland to live off Malcolm's riches."

As he expected, the blonde's eyes narrowed while she no doubt considered someone else getting their hands on all Malcolm's money. No matter how much she professed to love his stepson, Eldon knew it was the boy's fortune Melody loved the most. Her family didn't exactly wallow in poverty, but her father barely managed to hold on to his small mill, especially since Percy had died. Eldon had discovered Percy's agreement to a premium price for Parsons Mill fabric. He'd forced the board to put paid to that practice after his brother's death, and Parsons was now on the brink of bankruptcy.

"Of course I expected he'd come to his senses, eventually," Melody said airily. "I *was* a tad afraid he'd wait too long and she'd have her hooks into him. She certainly seems to have pulled the wool over Elizabeth's eyes."

Eldon nodded sympathetically. "Yes, I'm afraid my wife is far too prone to pick up wayward strays. I don't mind so much when it's a kitten, but a scheming young woman is another matter entirely. I had thought it time to suggest Malcolm take a more prominent role in the company, but if he can't see past the red head's wiles, I'm not sure he can handle the job." He bit back a smile as her expression grew calculating.

"Malcolm needed a little time. Now he's back home, I'm certain he'll see everything more clearly." She smirked, all but licking her lips as she twirled a loose strand of hair around her finger.

Eldon nodded. "I'm sure you're right. And he has his friends to help him." He looked at Melody and inclined his head. "You've always been such a positive influence, dear. I think you need to take a firm hand and guide him in the correct direction."

"Me? Why, whatever can I do? The engagement party is tonight."

"The party is still on, of course, but I don't think it would take much to turn it into a welcome home party for Malcolm and Elizabeth, and relegate Bree to a secondary role as just another survivor of the *Titanic* tragedy. Especially since Malcolm already wants to distance himself from her, now he's seen you again."

Melody smiled as she turned her head so she could see herself in a large mirror on the far wall. "He did seem quite happy to see me, until the chit grabbed onto him as tightly as a barnacle." She patted her coiffure and said airily, "I suppose as a friend, it is my duty to help save him from an unfortunate situation."

Eldon tipped his head. "Good. I'm glad you're willing to help. Tonight, as early as possible, I'd like you to take Malcolm out to the garden. I don't care what you tell him--just get him to go out there with you. I'm sure you'll know what to do when you have him to yourself in the moonlight." He raised an eyebrow questioningly.

She gave him a sultry smile. "I think I can manage to keep him occupied."

He stood. "Excellent. I'll do my best to keep the girl away from Malcolm and give you time to help him see the error of his ways. I think Elizabeth will be quite willing to help, as well. She's getting tired of Bree's demands to be treated like mistress of the house." He nodded briefly and said, "No need to see me out. I look forward to seeing you tonight, and your certain success."

Eldon left her seated, eyes narrowed, chewing on her index

finger. As he walked down the slate path, he congratulated himself on the first part of his plan. By the end of the evening, he would have everything he wanted: Bree, the family company and a funeral to plan for his stepson.

Chapter 33

Malcolm sped down the lane, enjoying the feel of wind whipping past his face. He was thankful he'd installed the small round windshield on the steering column, especially after a particularly large bug splattered against it. It reminded him of the first day home with Bree and her concerns about bugs, but his mind quickly shifted to their incredible night together. *And to think I've an endless number of similar nights to look forward to.*

He pulled to a stop outside Caleb's store. He knew there were many items for sale that weren't in the window or a display case. Teddy met him at the counter.

"Young Mr. DuMont, what brings you back into town? Your mother has purchased enough for three parties. There can't be anything she missed?" Teddy smiled.

"No, I think she has things well in hand. I'm searching for something special."

The woman's eyes lit up. "Something special, eh? It wouldn't be for that pretty thing you brought in a while back would it?"

211

Malcolm smiled and nodded. "I'd like a special gift for the engagement. I'll give her the same ring Father gave Mother, but I want something I chose too. Have you got anything tucked away that might fit the bill?"

Teddy rested a dimpled elbow on her palm and laid her index finger along her chin. "I might. I just might. Come along with me." She led the way through an arched entry to a long hall, bustling into an office on the right. A big safe crouched in the corner, a decorative painting and the name *LW Collins* in gold script gracing the front. Huge iron caster wheels had worn craters in the wood floor. It appeared it could resist a case of dynamite.

Keeping between Malcolm and the safe, Teddy twirled the dial back and forth until he heard an audible click, then she turned a lever and swung the door open on protesting hinges. The shopkeeper stepped to the side to reveal several cubbyholes stuffed with boxes, burlap bags and paper sacks. She made a variety of faces as she poked around in first one, then another of the cubbyholes, muttering to herself.

"Aha. I knew it was here somewhere. Been saving it for the proper occasion," Teddy said as she drew out a burlap-wrapped bundle and untied the length of twine holding it closed. With a flourish, she tipped the article out. Metal glittered in the sunlight streaming through the window, and the large opaque green stone in the middle of the antique brooch seemed to glow with an unearthly light.

"It's beautiful. What kind of stone is it?" Malcolm was already sold on taking the piece home.

Teddy ran her large index finger over the polished rock. "It's called chrysoprase. It's quite rare. I've had it for a long time. The feller I bought it from said it had magic powers or some such, and I have to admit it does make me feel a bit happier to look at it. It always seems a mite warm to the touch too."

"May I?" he asked. At her nod, Malcolm picked up the large piece, and indeed, felt warmth in his palm. The mint-green oval stone was almost two inches across, flanked by ornately styled wings of heavy gold filigree. Three diamonds, a large center one and two smaller, matching ones, connected the wings top and bottom.

"The stone is supposed to bring good luck," Teddy said, and added with a smile and rosy cheeks, "and fertility."

Malcolm felt his own face heat, matching the warmth in his hand. "I'll take it, Teddy, and I'll be happy whether or not it lives up to its reputation."

She nodded and folded it back into the sacking. "Will you be wanting it wrapped in a nice box? I can fix it all up for you and bring it with me tonight."

"That would be fine, if it's not too much trouble." He bussed her cheek and she waved him down the hall.

"Off with you, you young rascal."

As Malcolm went back outside, a distinct bounce in his step now he'd found the perfect engagement gift, he wondered what the price might be, then shrugged. Teddy wouldn't have shown him anything too expensive without telling him. She'd send an accounting at the end of the month, along with the party costs.

Malcolm spent the rest of the day checking in at several of the mills. One of the finishing plants had tested a new dye process, with pleasing results. He stuck a paper-wrapped bolt of the fabric in the passenger seat of the car to show his mother then checked his pocket watch for the hundredth time. With a sigh of relief, he saw it was late enough to return home without being sent away again. He was anxious to see Bree--and his mother, of course.

Chapter 34

After a hectic morning, Elizabeth decreed they were done with preparations. In a firm tone, she ordered her almost-daughter-in-law to bed for a recuperative nap, expressing her intent to do the same.

Bree lay in the big bed, her eyes closed. Memories of Malcolm looming above her in this very same bed caused a tightening and wetness between her thighs. The feel of his warm hands as they caressed her was so vivid her eyes flew wide, half expecting him to be there. But she was alone in the room. The windows were open and a fresh breeze stirred the lace curtains and brought the warble of bird songs to her ears.

She rolled onto her stomach, dragging the pillow that had lain under Malcolm's head to her cheek. She fancied it held a trace of his musky cologne. Her arms slipped around the crisp linen case and she clutched it to her breasts, wishing for a living, breathing, loving Malcolm to clasp. *Soon.* Her eyes closed and she drifted off to sleep.

* * * *

A light knock on the door a few hours later roused her and she called out, "Come in."

The young maid giggled with high spirits as she helped Bree bathe, then styled her hair and helped her into the satin gown. "Oh, my lord, Miss Bree. Aren't you a sight!" Hannah gushed.

"Thank you. You've done a wonderful job." Bree inspected herself critically in the full-length mirror, fearing she wouldn't stand up to the scrutiny of Malcolm and Elizabeth's friends. Her thick auburn hair was piled high on her head, lending the illusion of height. The gown Elizabeth had designed fit like a glove at the sheer shoulders and sleeves. Shimmering caramel silk draped softly to the floor, trimmed in delicate ivory lace. A novel tassel gathered the gown's hem, exposing an ivory underskirt which allowed Bree to walk easily despite the tight hobble design. For modesty's sake, Bree had added a scrap of lace in the deep V of the plunging neckline. Tucks and folds accented the bodice, with more lace ringing the lower edges of the waist banding. Another tassel weighted the draped silk down until it puddled near her waist in the back and exposed a considerable amount of creamy skin. Tan leather tango shoes with crisscrossed ankle straps and a low, curved heel encased her feet. Pale ivory silk stockings were held with garters below her knees. Three strands of iridescent pearls graced her neck and matching drop earrings nearly brushed her shoulders. Hannah pinned a small spray of pearls into her coiffure.

Bree bit her lip. "I hope they like me."

Bree realized she'd muttered the words out loud when Hannah protested. "Not like you? Not likely, I say. They're going to love you just like Master Malcolm does...and the rest of us too," she added shyly.

Bree hugged the young woman and sent her on her way with the admonishment to get some rest. Bree knew Elizabeth had exempted Hannah from work during the party after the maid toiled nearly nonstop the past several days.

Voices drifted in from the open window and she stepped over, hiding behind the drapes and gazing down. Guests already strolled along the graveled paths. Bree swallowed the lump that formed in her throat. What if the DuMonts' friends didn't like her? Would Malcolm decide he'd made a horrible mistake? Their lives were so different. He might tell Melody his fiancée came from wealth and power, but he knew it wasn't true. Instead, he would be saddled with an Irish country girl with a drunkard for a father and not even a pence to her name.

Bree hugged herself, unable to chase away the fear gnawing at her soul. She didn't belong here. It was only a matter of time before Malcolm realized it. She couldn't bear the thought he might look at her with dread and loathing some day. She found herself pacing the room, wracked with images of walking away from the beautiful house, Melody standing on the doorstep next to Malcolm, his arm draped around her.

She jumped as someone rapped on the door. "C-c-come in," she stuttered, half expecting a servant to escort her from the premises.

Elizabeth swept into the room, her face lighting up when she saw Bree in her party dress. "Oh, you're just lovely, dear." She circled

Terri Benson

Bree, reaching out to twitch a fold of lace into place. "Absolutely lovely!"

Bree sighed deeply. "The gown *is* beautiful, Elizabeth. Thank you."

Elizabeth laughed and patted Bree on the shoulder. "I wasn't talking about the gown, dear. And don't thank me. You did all the work. As a matter of fact, thank you for *my* gown. It's a perfect fit."

The older woman pirouetted gracefully, showing off the loose over jacket of lavender velvet, which hung in heavy folds from wide lapels and loose sleeves to a handkerchief hem at knee length. Bree knew the tightly fitted dark purple silk sheath underneath clung to Elizabeth's curves. A jaunty cap with purple dyed marabou feathers sat precariously above one eye. An antique marcasite-and-amethyst setting graced her neck and ears.

"I think it's time for our grand entrance. I saw Malcolm come home about an hour ago and I heard his voice downstairs as I came down the hall. Shall we?"

Elizabeth crooked her elbow and Bree slipped her arm in. They marched out into the hall and to the top of the stairs.

Bree stumbled to a halt. She gazed down at the sea of color filling the large foyer and spilling into side rooms. The women hadn't made a sound but, as if sensing their presence, faces below turned up to stare.

Bridge blinked and bit her lip, turning in dismay to Elizabeth. The older woman reached up and squeezed her hand. "Steady now, dear. You're the belle of the ball tonight. They want to see what a lucky

218

man my son is."

Reassured, Bree matched her steps to Elizabeth as they descended the wide, curved staircase. Malcolm appeared, a broad smile lighting his face. He bounded up a few steps and reached to take Bree's hand as they drew near. Elizabeth relinquished her arm and took a few more steps before she stopped to address her guests.

"Welcome, everyone. It's so lovely to see you all. I'd like to introduce you to this beautiful young woman, Bree Barry, without whom I would not be standing here."

A long, loud round of applause rippled across the room, amid cheers of "Here, here." Malcolm tucked Bree's arm in his, and they followed Elizabeth down the stairs.

Bree smiled and nodded to the blur of faces crowding near, but couldn't help noticing there had been no mention of wedding plans in Elizabeth's introduction.

Chapter 35

Bree was pulled away from Malcolm almost immediately by Teddy, who insisted on introducing her to a group of elderly couples. From then on she was passed from group to group, occasionally catching a glimpse of Malcolm. He always seemed to have a beautiful young woman--or two--at his side. And yet, a smile lit his face each time their gazes met.

When they eventually reunited, Malcolm steered her to a secluded alcove. "Wait right here. I'll get us some wine." He paused and looked at her intently. "I have something very important I want to talk to you about, but you've been so busy with introductions we haven't had a moment together." He gave her a long, clinging kiss on the temple, his hand cupping the back of her neck as his thumb stroked under her ear. With a reluctant sigh, he pulled away and dodged through the tightly packed bodies toward a table set up with cases of wine and hard liquor.

He was gone an awfully long time.

* * * *

"Having a nice time, are we?"

Bree startled violently and a frisson of revulsion zipped down her back at the sound of Eldon's low voice. She glanced over her shoulder. He leaned against the wall, his casual stance telling her Malcolm couldn't be anywhere near. Eldon was tall enough to easily see over the mass of people and wouldn't be so relaxed if there was any chance of a confrontation with his stepson.

"I was."

He chuckled at her tone.

"Malcolm will be back in a moment, Eldon. After your behavior last night, I think it would be a good idea if you made yourself scarce. It would be horrible for Elizabeth if you and Malcolm got in a fight at her party."

"Fight? Malcolm and I? Not to worry. I explained about last night's misunderstanding. He knows I merely attempted to give you a fatherly peck on the cheek and, in your inexperience, you mistook it for something else. I am sorry about the fire, but Elizabeth assures me you suffered no real damage."

Bree sucked in her breath. The cad! Surely Malcolm didn't believe such a pack of lies? "If that's your idea of an apology, you've wasted your time. I'm quite certain of your intent and, truthfully, I would rather burn to death than suffer it." His cheek muscles flexed and his dark eyes narrowed a fraction, but his jovial smile seemed glued in place.

He regarded the crowd with disinterest. "I promised I wouldn't say anything, but I feel it's only fair I warn you. You may regret your comments very soon, dear, once you realize I may be the only one who has any intentions for you."

She turned in her seat to face him, puzzled by his words.

He leered down at her and continued, snide amusement in his voice, "I think you'll find America a very inhospitable place for a young woman on her own. No money. No family. Bad things happen."

"Lucky for me I won't be on my own." Bree turned away, hoping Eldon would leave her in peace. Where was Malcolm? He'd been gone much longer than necessary to get wine.

Eldon noticed her intent gaze. "He's not there, you know. I saw him go out to the garden a few moments ago with a woman. I'm not sure, but I believe it might have been the as-always lovely Melody. I came upon them today while out riding. They were very cozy in that shaded little glade until they realized I was there. Their hurried excuses were rather amusing. As if I cared what they did in private."

Bree couldn't help it. She swiveled around and stared up at him. She wanted to call him a liar. Wanted to tell him to leave her be. That Malcolm wouldn't do that. He couldn't! She bit her lip as her hands twisted her long satin gloves into a knot.

He gave her a sympathetic look, and she was almost convinced he meant it. "I don't think it's right for them to pick up where they left off without explaining it to you. Even if the engagement is off." He paused at her gasp then continued with a smirk. "You didn't know? Oh, my. I am sorry. I assumed Malcolm would discuss it with you *before* the party. Well, considering the dishabille I found the two of them in earlier, he probably didn't have time to do more than clean up before the guests started arriving. I'm sure he'll talk to you very soon. Now, much as I've enjoyed our little chat, I do have other guests to entertain. But not Melody--I think Malcolm has her well in hand." Eldon chuckled at his joke and sauntered off.

Bree slumped in her chair. She couldn't, wouldn't believe it. Malcolm had likely been detained by a friend. Eldon was just trying to upset her. Malcolm loved her. Didn't he? But he *had* mentioned he had something important to talk to her about. And if he and Melody really were together, maybe Eldon had told the truth. Needing to be alone to think, Bree quickly stood and walked down the hall to the library. The door was closed, discouraging guests from entering, and she found it empty. She crossed the room slowly to the trio of tall floor-to-ceiling doors, mates to those in the parlor. Flaming torches lit the garden at intervals and light spilled into the darkened room through the undraped windows. At first glance the garden was empty, the cool breeze and hunger having driven the guests indoors, but then she caught a flicker of movement.

A pair of figures stood close together at the edge of the torch glow--the man, taller than average and the woman with hair gleaming gold in the firelight. Even though she couldn't see his face, Bree knew it was Malcolm held so tightly in the blonde's embrace, Malcolm's head dipping down to the pale upturned face. It *was* true. Malcolm had chosen Melody. She truly was alone again. The dream of a new start in a new land was turning into a nightmare.

As tears coursed unheeded down her cheeks, Bree fled to the

hallway, instinctively turning away from the noise of the party. A few yards down the parquet floor the door to the working areas of the house yielded to her urgent flight. Head bent to shield it from the startled cook, Bertie, and the servers working in the kitchen, she hurried across the room. Bree passed through the open door to the porch then pushed through the swinging screen door. In her haste, she nearly missed the step down to the lawn, and if not for the sudden appearance of Carlisle at her elbow, might have fallen ignominiously on her face.

"Here, now, miss. That could have been a bad tumble." He looked into her tear-stained face. "Are you all right? Should I call the missus?"

Bree shook her head, trying to stifle the sobs threatening to escape. "N-n-no, thank you, Carlisle. I needed some fresh air."

"Umm, if you... Well, I'm going into town to fetch a few more cases of, umm, wine. Yes, that's right. A few cases of wine. If you'd like to go anywhere, I'd be glad to take you. It's a lovely evening. You ever ride in Rolls Royce? Oh, yeah, 'course you did. When I brought you from the station." He glanced around, as if he were searching for something.

Bree was surprised at his eagerness to take her for a ride. But she looked closer and saw a deep blush on his clean-shaven cheeks. He was a nice young man, a bit simple perhaps, but always polite. Her sudden arrival had obviously embarrassed him. She started to offer a polite refusal when a possible escape from her impossible situation came to mind.

"Yes, thank you, Carlisle. I think I would like to go to town. Do you know the schedule at the station? I forgot I need to visit my aunt in Boston, to...well, to tell her about Malcolm. With all the excitement, it slipped my mind. She'd be so upset if I don't explain. I'll just run up and get my reticule." Bree hesitated. If she went back into the house someone would ask questions, or worse yet, she'd run into Malcolm and Melody. She couldn't face them.

Carlisle frowned and tapped his chin, then said, "There's a train leaves in about an hour."

She jumped as another deep voice spoke from the darkness.

Chapter 36

Fred Dunby watched the group from his perch in the big oak tree. He recognized the pretty copper-haired girl as the itty bitty thing he'd seen at the station and later through the window. The young man with her was vaguely familiar. The third party, although hidden in shadow, was his quarry.

Fred had rented a horse and ridden to the estate earlier in the afternoon. It had been an unpleasant trip to say the least. As a sailor, he'd never had much use for horses, and even less skill. The nag had nearly unseated him several times, even though the man at the stables swore Peanut was as mild-mannered as they came. He sat, motionless, as Eldon strode out of the shadows.

"Is there a problem, my dear?" Eldon asked the girl.

"No, I... I'm going into town with Carlisle. It's stuffy inside and I'd like some fresh air."

The uniformed man whipped off his cap and added, "Miss Bree wants to visit her aunt in Boston, but don't have any money with her for a ticket. She's going to get her bag."

Fred thought it odd the man explained this to DuMont, especially when it didn't seem any of his business. He saw the gleam of white teeth as Eldon smiled and reached into his coat pocket. He handed Carlisle something.

"See that she gets where she needs to go, Carl." He turned to the woman, "It's more than you'll need for the ticket, my dear. You can use it for food and such *on the way to your aunt's,*" he said in an amused tone. He turned with a chuckle and walked away, entering the barn across the yard.

The two stood where he'd left them. Soon the young man started fidgeting.

"If you want to make the train, miss, we'll need to leave right away. It's a fair piece and I have to slow down in the dark. We have a lot of deer around here."

Bree nodded and followed him to the car. He held the door for her so she could climb into the back seat, then jogged around to the front and started the car. They crept slowly down the drive, the big engine rumbling quietly.

Fred was about to climb down and search for Eldon when another car started in the barn and rolled out. Headlights dark, the car followed leisurely along some distance behind the Rolls. From light spilling out a window at the back of the house, Fred recognized Eldon at the wheel. As soon as the car passed behind a shrub, he scrambled out of the tree and raced toward Peanut. It took him two tries to hoist himself up into the saddle. In his haste to keep the car in sight, Fred kicked the surprised animal repeatedly while jerking the reins first one way then another. The horse eventually took the bit in his teeth and cantered down the lane toward home.

Fred heard the throaty grumble of the Rolls from around a turn ahead, and stopped. The horse immediately dropped his head and began munching grass growing from the middle of the road. He slipped out of the saddle and crept closer. Voices carried through the night air.

"Mr. Eldon? Sir? I don't think I like this. The miss here don't want to go with you. You told me to take her to town and that's all right 'cause that's what she said she wanted to do. But she don't want to go with--."

The man's voice cut off abruptly, followed by an odd, watery thud. The woman screamed, and was quickly muffled. Before Fred could follow the road around a thick stand of trees, an engine roared to life and he heard pebbles ricocheting off bark and rocks as they were thrown from beneath the tires. He hurried around the corner, and watched the smaller car speed away. The big Rolls sat by the side of the road, the engine idling softly. A black lump lay in the dirt beside the open back door. Fred crept closer.

"Blimey, not again!" he muttered. The lump was the young man. He sprawled on his side, head turned away. A horrendous dent distorted the side of his face. Blood and something more solid glistened in the moonlight. A tire iron lay nearby. With a grimace of revulsion, Fred turned away, noticing the empty back seat of the car. The young woman was nowhere to be seen. He turned and ran for Peanut. He made it into the saddle in one try, and soon the startled

228

animal galloped down the road as he clung frantically to saddle horn and mane. He rode into Eldon's dust on the outskirts of town and reined the horse to a bone-jangling trot so he wouldn't overtake his quarry. The small lights on the rear of the car helped him follow as it steered into an alley. It continued straight into the black maw of an open, two-story carriage house. A moment later Eldon appeared and pulled the doors shut, the lock snapping loudly in the stillness of the night. A lamp was lit inside, sending out a pale flickering glow.

Fred dismounted and tethered Peanut to a convenient downspout, then sidled up next to the garage, careful to stay away from the windows. He heard a car door open and close. A muffled cry rang out, followed by the sound of a sharp slap. Footsteps pounded on stairs. The light moved higher and the lower level faded to a dark gray. Fred risked a quick glance through the small, barred window. The car, glinting in the dull moonlight, sat in the middle of the dirt floor, the engine ticking as it cooled.

Chewing his cheek, he wondered, *What now?*

Chapter 37

"What are you doing, Melody? Have you lost your mind?" Malcolm shoved her back in disgust, trying to untangle her arms from his neck. "I only agreed to come out here because you said you needed to talk to me urgently about your father's business, although I thought we settled everything yesterday morning. Obviously, it was a ruse. I'm going back in. I think it's best if you sit with your parents, and please don't come to the house again unless you're invited by someone other than Eldon."

Malcolm spun on his heel, but before he took a step, Melody cried, "I don't understand. If you're not going to marry that Irish girl, what's wrong with me? You used to like kissing me."

He turned back, surprised at the piteous tone in Melody's normally demanding voice.

Then he realized what she said. "What do you mean, 'Now that I'm not going to marry Bree'? Of course I'm going to marry her. This is an engagement party, remember?"

"But Eldon said you'd changed your mind. That you realized you wanted me and you're going to send her home."

Eldon--the bastard-- was still trying to stir up trouble. Well, enough was enough. "Melody, go home. I think of you as an old friend, nothing more. I intend to marry Bree because I love her. You've allowed Eldon to feed you lies, even though you're smart enough to know better. I'll talk to your father in a day or so about the mill. I don't intend to let him lose it--Father wouldn't have wanted that. You don't need to marry me to save it, so find someone who loves you."

This time, he kept walking. The sound of Melody's sobs followed him down the path, but the need to talk to Bree was far more important than soothing a spoiled woman's feelings.

Malcolm headed to the alcove where he'd left his fiancée, but the chairs were empty. He asked everyone standing nearby if they'd seen her leave. The blank or curious stares he received in return were answer enough. This didn't feel right. Malcolm was sure Eldon was up to more than just causing a rift between him and Bree, and the thought caused a painful contraction in his chest. He followed the hallway, opening doors as he came to them. When he looked across the library and realized he could see Melody framed by the middle pane of windows, a flash of guilt jolted through him, followed by a feeling of dread. He pushed open the door at the end of the hall and entered the kitchen. Controlled mayhem confronted him as Bertie and her assistants bustled around the room, dodging servers loading heavy silver platters and trays with food and drinks. There was a loud crash and the sound of breaking glass as two men collided. Bertie swore like a drayman.

He surveyed the kitchen but saw no sign of Bree. Malcolm started to turn back when a scullery maid tentatively approached him, plucking at his sleeve. "Sir? The little miss. Is she all right?"

He bent down to the maid, not more than thirteen or fourteen, the eldest daughter of Bertie. "What do you mean?"

The girl appeared ready to bolt but managed to stammer out, "The miss. She looked like she was crying."

Malcolm grabbed her by the shoulders but quickly let go as sheer panic filled her eyes. He took a calming breath and asked quietly, "When did you see her?"

"Just a bit ago. She went out back. I checked a few minutes later, but she was gone."

Malcolm heard the last part of the sentence over his shoulder as he slammed through the screen door into the night.

* * * *

The yard was empty. Silent as a grave. Seeing no sign of Bree, he turned to the barn. Perhaps she'd gone to see Murray. Maybe her legs hurt and she went for more salve? Malcolm's feet moved faster across the hard-packed dirt.

There were only a few lanterns burning in the massive building, giving off a faint, smoky light that cast deep shadows. "Bree?" he called, running more than walking now. "Bree, are you there, love?"

Silence.

He was only a few stalls from the far end when one of the half doors swung into his path. He barely managed to stop as Murray

232

stepped out.

"What's the hurry, boy? You and that pretty miss playing hide-n-seek?" Murray's face crinkled in amusement at his joke.

"Have you seen Bree? They said she came out into the yard, but I can't find her."

The smile slipped from Murray's face. "She's not here. I ain't seen her." The old man seemed to sense Malcolm's growing panic.

He spun away, thinking frantically of where else he should search. The groom called after him, "Carl took the big car out, and Mr. Eldon took the Pierce Arrow right after. They ain't been gone more 'n ten minutes or so, but I didn't see your girl."

Malcolm stopped in his tracks. Eldon drove the Arrow? Why would Eldon take his car when Carlisle drove the Rolls? He was more convinced than ever Eldon was up to something that did not bode well for Bree.

In a few long strides, Malcolm was at the Mercer. He quickly made the necessary adjustments and cranked the car. With a throaty roar that left the barn full of horses kicking and prancing, and would certainly earn him a dressing down from Murray, he accelerated out into the lane. He pushed the car as fast as he dared, the small electric headlamps barely piercing the darkness. As the car slewed around a corner, Malcolm wrenched the brake handle and careened across the road to avoid hitting a car parked half on and half off the roadway. The racecar bounced down a small embankment and barely missed a big maple before rattling to a stop. He shook his head to clear it from the wild ride, then shifted into reverse and powered the car back up to the road. As he braked hard the car skidded around, its feeble lights illuminated a prone body lying in a pool of dark liquid next to the Rolls' open door. With a heavy weight in his chest, Malcolm climbed out and knelt next to Carlisle's body. A quick touch confirmed the man was dead. Malcolm stepped around to the Rolls and climbed into the back seat, his heart pounding. No small, copper-headed body sprawled lifelessly on the broad bench seat. Thank God! The weight in his chest eased a tiny bit.

A pale object caught his eye and he reached down to pick up a caramel-colored tassel with a small scrap of ivory lace still attached. Tighter than ever, the band of fear crushed his breath. Bree was in trouble. Since Eldon followed Carlisle and the lane didn't have any place wide enough to pass the big car, his stepfather couldn't have missed the Rolls Royce, even in the dark. Bree wasn't physically capable of hurting a man of Carlisle's size--but Eldon was.

Regretfully leaving the chauffer lying in the road, Malcolm ignored the door and leaped over the side of the sports car, slamming it into gear as soon as his feet touched the pedals, and pushed the Mercer to its maximum speed. He was forced to slow as he entered the town proper, using his horn when required to warn slow-moving carriages as he overtook them. Angry shouts echoed behind, but he ignored them.

Up and down the grid-like streets he cruised, checking each glint of metal for Eldon's Pierce Arrow. He completed a full circuit and came back to the start. "Damn!" Malcolm cried, pounding his fist on the steering wheel. If Eldon hadn't stopped in town, he could be half-

way to Boston or several other cities. There was no way of telling.
Slumping in despair, he let his head fall back, eyes closed. The vision
of Bree, a hurt, reproachful expression on her face, filled his head.
What had he done?

"Mebbe I can help."

Malcolm jerked as he heard the Cockney accent.

Chapter 38

As Eldon held the thrashing hellcat in his arms, he had a moment to wonder if he'd bitten off more than he could chew. Slapping Bree when she'd tried to escape downstairs hadn't had the effect he had expected. Instead of cowering from him, she'd come at him, nails slashing at his face, feet kicking at his shins. It took all his strength to hold her off. He knew he could easily have knocked her out, but he didn't want to damage her pretty face. And, more importantly, he wanted her wide awake when he began her education in bed. He looked across the warped floorboards to the tarnished brass bed in the corner and smiled. He'd put clean sheets on it himself earlier today in preparation for Bree's "classes." She probably wouldn't appreciate the fact he wouldn't have considered such menial labor for anyone but her. He expected proper thanks for his efforts--or perhaps, *improper* thanks.

The back of Bree's head slammed against his chest with enough forced to nearly knock the breath out of him. Who would have expected such a small package to have such potent strength? Damn that stupid Carlisle. He'd followed orders to get Bree away from the house, but then he'd gotten cold feet. Eldon could use another pair of hands to control the hot-headed minx. Instead, the fool had tried to play Sir Galahad.

Eldon automatically countered Bree's struggles as he sorted through options. It would have been wiser to speed through town and get as far away as possible, considering it wouldn't take long for someone leaving the party to find the Rolls and Carlisle's body. But, then again, it was unlikely anyone had seen the three of them together. There would be too many questions and confusion for anyone to come hunting for him right away. It hadn't come off exactly as he'd planned, but he'd gone to so much trouble to put together his secret hideaway, he was damn well going to use it.

It never ceased to amaze Eldon that people wanted to believe him, no matter the evidence or how odd the circumstances--even more so now he was rich. No one ever connected the dots in the past. Not as a child when animals kept turning up mutilated and dead, not after his poor brother died so suddenly, not when the company accountant disappeared with all that money and, of course, not when his wife's devoted maid absconded in Europe. The stupid bitch thought she could blackmail him when she caught him adding the powder to Elizabeth's morning tea. Eleanor's disappearance hadn't even raised an eyebrow. He was probably the only one who missed her, and only because she had been somewhat amusing in bed. He'd tired of her, anyway.

Eldon glanced down at the coppery head pummeling his chest. To spare himself any more bruises, he placed his hand over her mouth and nose and held it until her struggles weakened. Just when he thought Bree sufficiently subdued, sharp teeth sank into the flesh beneath his thumb. He twisted his other hand in her tangle of hair and yanked her head back, staring down into flashing green eyes. "You little hellion! I'm going to enjoy repaying you for every single bruise and scratch." His hand throbbed, but the engorged mass between his legs throbbed even harder. He needed to bed the girl right now, tonight. Until he got that out of his system, they weren't going anywhere.

He instinctively peered out the lone upstairs window. Across the alley loomed the big three-story house where he'd spent so many pleasurable hours with the young women cloistered there. The proprietress catered to his somewhat unusual proclivities to keep his profitable custom--he'd spent a great deal of money there. The women were expected to accede to his every demand. He could do anything he wanted, short of committing murder. Now he would have his very own concubine. One that he would take great pleasure in teaching how to satisfy his whims. Eldon caught his reflection in the glass and turned his head side to side, admiring the way his long, dark hair curled against his collar, the distinguished streaks of gray at his temples. He was still a handsome devil, although he detected the beginnings of bags under his eyes.

Bree's hip swinging hard against his swollen groin disrupted his preening. He gasped in pain and ecstasy. *Soon, my fiery Irish lass. Soon.*

Even as Eldon's hands roved Bree's luscious body, he planned how he would keep suspicion away. As long as he kept the girl out of sight, he could bluff his way through. He'd rented the coach house under an assumed name weeks ago, as soon as they returned from Europe, anticipating the need for a private sanctuary. He'd avoided using the building until today and was certain he could keep Bree hidden here indefinitely if he was careful. Then, when the excitement died down, he'd take her to the city where it would be easy to conceal her until she was sufficiently under control. A smile lit his face. *I might even be able to come up with some way for Malcolm to take the blame for her disappearance.* He enjoyed the thought until a sharp heel skewered his instep.

Chapter 39

Malcolm peered into the darkness as the speaker stepped closer. It was the red-headed man from the train station who'd accused Eldon of murder. At the time, he had been sure the man was insane. "What do you want?"

"'Ere, now. That's no way to talk to the only man who can help you and the miss, now is it?"

"Bree? You know where she is?" Malcolm eyed him closely. There was no proof the man hadn't taken her himself. Maybe Eldon wasn't even involved.

"That's the name. That's what 'e called her. The pretty Irish lass from the station. Aye, I know where she is. And I know the bloke what's got her. He's a killer, he is. She don't have no chance if'n we don't help her right quick-like."

Malcolm stared hard into the pale eyes glinting in the low light. Dunson? No, wait, Dunby. Fred Dunby. With no real choice in the matter, Malcolm said, "Get in. Where are they?"

"You don't need the car. They's down there, in a carriage house."

240

Fred jerked his thumb over his shoulder.

Malcolm steered to the side of the road and switched off the car. The other man started down the dark alley at a good clip and Malcolm hurried to catch up. He stayed a step or two behind, still not entirely convinced of the man's innocence. "How do you know they're here?" he asked suspiciously.

"Shhh," Fred said, finger to his lips. He pointed to a weathered story-and-a-half structure. The lower side window was barred and dark, and the upper gable end a solid wall with worn fish-scale shingles. "I been doggin' him ever since I saw him at the station in New York. I was out there at the house watchin' when he followed the girl in the big car tonight. I wanted to find out what he was up to. Then I come across the dead fellow in the road and the big bastard lit out with the girl. He drove the blue car in there, with her. I heard her scream."

Malcolm stiffened. "What happened? What did he do?"

He felt rather than saw the man shrug. "Dunno. I heard a slap and mumbling and cursing then they went up some stairs. But I know what he's capable of. I watched him shoot an officer on the *Titanic* without even blinking an eye. He would'da killed me too, if I hadn't let him in the lifeboat. He said Timmy told him the other blokes found different lifeboats, but seein' how they didn't hardly let any men in the boats, and I ain't been able to find Timmy, I been wonderin' about that too."

The memory of the *Titanic* officer who'd been shot, and the two bludgeoned men he'd found nearby--one a steward, the other a crony of Eldon's--flashed in Malcolm's mind. Then there was Carlisle. Fear for Bree and fury at Eldon's lethal bent sent adrenaline roiling though his veins. Malcolm reached for the door.

Fred put his hand on Malcolm's arm. "It's locked. I already checked."

He tested the latch anyway. Through a narrow gap between the doors, he saw a chain and padlock. He walked over to the corner and peered around--another barred window. As he turned back, his jacket snagged on a piece of metal. It was one of three heavy iron hinges pinning the door at the corner of the building.

Malcolm smiled grimly. He jogged silently back to the car and retrieved the custom-made toolbox from under the passenger seat. Back at the coach house, with Fred breathing nasally beside him, he used a big screwdriver to lever the pin out of the lower two hinges. He couldn't reach the topmost one, but when he tugged the doors below the metal flanges, he found the old wood rotted at the bottom. The two of them were able to pull the lower edge of the door away from the building enough to crawl through.

Inside the dark carriage house, they moved carefully around the car, avoiding trash strewn about the floor. Scrapes, thuds and muttered curses echoed from upstairs. It was hard to hold back, but Malcolm worried he might cause Bree more injury if he ran up the stairs without knowing what he would be dealing with. The first tread of the stairs creaked loudly, and a yelp from upstairs was abruptly cut off. Malcolm gave up on caution and bolted up the rickety flight. He burst through the door at the top of the stairs--and skidded to a halt.

Chapter 40

Elizabeth was quite peeved. It was time for the big announcement, and neither Bree nor Malcolm was anywhere to be found. Her son had insisted the engagement announcement be a big surprise, complete with toasts and dancing. It wasn't like him to be so cavalier about such a carefully planned schedule. She certainly didn't begrudge the pair time together, but their guests were waiting and, once married, Malcolm and Bree had a whole lifetime ahead of them. Thinking they might have stolen into the garden, Elizabeth stepped off the terrace and took the wide graveled path. She investigated a few dark niches most often occupied, but they were empty. The night air was cool and the guests had retreated to the house. She was about to do the same when she heard rustling and muttering on the other side of the shrubbery. With a sigh of relief, she stepped around and was surprised to find Melody sitting by herself, sniffling and dabbing at her nose with a hanky.

"Whatever are you doing out here, Melody? It's gotten quite cool.

You'll catch your death." The girl didn't answer, just sniveled louder. Out of patience, the older woman said, "Have you seen Malcolm and Bree?"

Elizabeth was shocked when Melody burst into loud sobs and covered her face with her hands. She sat on the stone bench beside the blonde. "What is it, dear? Are you ill? Shall I call your mother?"

Through hiccupping sobs, Melody managed to say, "No, Elizabeth. I'm all right. Just incredibly stupid and naïve. And embarrassed. Do you think Malcolm will ever forgive me?"

"Malcolm forgive you? Whatever for?" Elizabeth asked, mystified.

Melody raised her head, dabbed at red, swollen eyes, and blew her noise loudly. "I've been a fool. Eldon told me Malcolm didn't want Bridget--he wanted me--and I believed him. I acted, well..." The young woman's face darkened in the faint light. "I acted very badly."

"Wait. You said Eldon told you Malcolm wasn't going to marry Bridget? When was that?"

"This afternoon. He stopped by the house and said if I got Malcolm alone, I could get him back."

"When did you speak with Malcolm?" Elizabeth's impatience returned. She sensed something was very wrong, especially if Eldon was involved.

"A bit ago. He was very angry with me." Melody began to sob again.

Elizabeth said firmly, "That's enough. Dry your face and let's go inside. I need to find Eldon and Malcolm and Bridget and get to the bottom of this." She handed Melody another handkerchief and pulled her to her feet.

Once in the house, Elizabeth sent Melody off to the powder room to freshen up and sought the butler.

"Anderson, I need to find Eldon, Malcolm and Miss Bridget. All the servants need to look for them. It's very important." He held up his hand to stop her as she started to turn away.

"Cook just told me Miss Bridget and Mr. Malcolm went out back."

The two of them hustled down the hall, Elizabeth smiling and waving to the guests as if nothing was amiss.

In the kitchen, Anderson called Bertie to join them. The heavy-set woman complied, dragging a young girl along with her.

"Bertie, have you seen Malcolm and Miss Bridget?"

"Yes, ma'am. Amy here--" She nodded at her daughter. "She saw Miss Bridget go through, then a short while later, Mr. Malcolm. They both went out back."

Elizabeth immediately went to the screen door and into the backyard, the others trailing behind. She saw no sign of anyone. Just then lamplight wobbled from the barn, and the old groom stepped out. Elizabeth met him halfway.

"Have you seen Malcolm and Miss Bridget, Murray?"

"I saw Malcolm. He was huntin' for the miss. When he found out Carlisle took the Rolls and Mr. Eldon the Pierce, he took off after them like a bat outta hell in his little roadster. Pardon me, ma'am." He dipped his head in apology.

Elizabeth patted him absently on the arm. "No matter." She bit her lip. Why would Malcolm follow Eldon, who apparently followed Carlisle? And what about Bree? The sense of foreboding grew stronger. She turned and hurried into the house, heading for the parlor and a friend whom she knew would help.

Chapter 41

Malcolm stared across the room. Eldon and Bree stood facing him, his fiancée clutched tightly to his stepfather's chest. The large bore of a pistol pressed against her ear.

"Stop right there, Malcolm. Another step and your dearly beloved will become your dearly departed."

Malcolm halted, every muscle in his body rebelling.

Bree had been struggling when he first saw them, but now she stood stock still, her gaze glued to his face. He saw no fear. Instead, a magnificent anger burned in her blazing green eyes.

"Are you all right?" he asked, his voice hoarse with emotion.

The tiniest hint of a smiled flickered at the corners of her mouth and she gave a nod.

Eldon sneered. "She's perfectly fine...for now. I'm feeling so generous. I'll give you a chance to keep her that way. There's a pen and paper on the table there. I want you to write out a bank draft for two hundred fifty thousand dollars, payable to me. The money's already sitting in the account. The tidy sum I got when Percy's business manager 'disappeared' is long gone, so I recently liquidated a few assets to give me a bit more spending money. You can explain to the board of directors you wanted to give me some seed money for my new endeavor, since you'll also be giving me the mill in Uxbridge. You won't even miss it. In addition, you'll need to write out a statement saying Carlisle was trying to kidnap your fiancée and, in the struggle to save her, I was forced to kill him. I then brought her here and summoned you."

Malcolm considered Eldon's demands. Even if he wrote out the statements, they wouldn't stand up in court if he disputed them. Then he knew. Eldon had no intention of allowing him to live. Once the documents were signed, he would kill Malcolm, and probably Bree as well, so there would be no one to call him a liar.

Even as he nodded his agreement, Malcolm frantically worked to conceive a plan which ensured Bree's escape. He walked slowly to the table. Vellum scattered across the surface. It looked as if Eldon had been using the room to plan his most recent escapade. There were notes on the Uxbridge Mill and, most telling, several attempts to mimic Malcolm's signature. Even more convinced Eldon had no intention of letting him leave the room alive, Malcolm glanced over his shoulder to see if Eldon had made the mistake of moving within range. He hadn't.

"It appears you've thought this out very thoroughly, Eldon."

The older man smiled. "It's about time you realized how much superior I am to you when it comes to business and management. If Percy let me run the company, I would have done great things. You'll see. Well, perhaps not." He laughed, but the timbre was off and a shiver went down Malcolm's spine. *The man's insane!*

Malcolm pulled a piece of vellum toward him and picked up a pen, then slowly wrote the documents out. He fiddled with the pen nib in an attempt to stall before signing.

Eldon said conversationally, "You know, Malcolm, I really don't trust this Irish vixen, either. I think I'd like her signature on those as well. That way, neither of you can cause me any trouble." He motioned impatiently with the gun.

Malcolm penned his name at the bottom of the document as his mind worked furiously, desperately, to formulate a plan to keep Bree alive. He knew if she added her signature, it would be her death warrant.

"Now you." Eldon shoved Bree toward Malcolm. She stumbled and fell against his legs, blocking the planned lunge toward his stepfather. As Eldon raised the gun barrel until it centered on Malcolm's chest, an evil leer split his face.

Malcolm couldn't take his eyes off Bree, tormented by the thought this would be the last time he'd see her beautiful face. The pistol's deafening report reverberated in the small space. Shocked to feel no pain, he stared hard at Bree, looking for blood. She appeared confused and surprised, but not injured.

A clatter from the stairs drew their attention. Fred stood on the top step, a gun at his feet. Bright red spread over his chest as he gaped at them in shock. With a muttered curse, his knees buckled and he toppled over, rolling down the stairs to land below with a thud.

Malcolm spun back, seeing Eldon's gaze fixed on the stairs, his expression disinterested. With a roar of rage, he leaped. Eldon's reflexes were cat-like and the gun instantly returned, but Malcolm's momentum bowled Eldon over and they both crashed to the floor. The older man struggled to get the gun against any part of Malcolm, while Malcolm tried to wrest it from his hands.

Bree scampered out of the way, watching for an opening to help Malcolm. The gun went off, the echo mingling with her scream of anguish.

Chapter 42

Bree froze. Her heart pounded, her breath coming in gasps as the men struggled against each other on the floor, their limbs entangled. Eldon rolled away, the gun still in his hand, and struggled to his feet.

"God, no! Malcolm?" she moaned, throwing herself on her knees beside him. His vivid blue eyes stared up in shock.

"I'm fine, Bree. I'm not hurt," he said in an amazed tone.

They turned to Eldon. He frowned, looking down as he surveyed the scarlet stain spreading across his white shirt. The gun slipped from his hand and bounced on the floor. Eldon raised his head and glared at them, his expressing a mixture of confusion and fury. Then he crumpled and fell face first on the floorboards.

Bree helped Malcolm to his feet and they embraced. He held her so tightly she could barely breathe.

"I was so frightened when the gun went off and he got up." Sobs bubbled up and she sagged with relief in his arms.

"You can't have been any more frightened than when I saw you standing there with a gun at your head." She felt him shiver as he pulled her closer.

Bree gazed up at him. "Who was he? The man on the stairs. I know him from somewhere."

"The man at the station who accused Eldon of murder. Apparently he's been following us. If not for him, I never would have known where you were. I think he saved both our lives."

Arm in arm, they went down the stairs. Their hope that Fred had only been injured was dashed by the impossible angle of his neck. Even if the shot to his chest hadn't killed him, the broken neck had.

Malcolm slipped his arms around her again and pulled her tight. "I want you here always, Bree. Forever."

She smiled up at him. "It might be rather unpractical, but I'm game if you are. I think, though, right now I'd very much like to go home."

He laughed and bent down to kiss her deeply. He wheeled around at the sound of breaking glass from upstairs. He motioned for her to stay, but she pelted up the stairs right behind him. Eldon's body no longer lay on the floor and the pistol was gone. The one window in the room, in the gable opposite the big doors downstairs, was shattered. Malcolm leaned out, but quickly ducked down with a curse as a bullet whizzed by and buried itself in the ceiling.

Bree grabbed his arm and hauled him away from the window.

Malcolm hugged her. "It's all right. He's running away as fast as he can. There's a lean-to below the window. Apparently he jumped or lowered himself down to it and then to the ground."

"Then he's still out there. With a gun. Oh, Malcolm," Bree cried.

"Let's go back to The Dell. We can deal with him better from there."

Chapter 43

Eldon swerved behind the corner of a building fifty yards from the carriage house, surprised no light appeared in any nearby window. A dog barked and he expected it wouldn't be long before someone came to investigate the shots. He peered up the pitch-black alley, but couldn't see Malcolm's silhouette in the window any longer. Movement on the ground drew his gaze. Two figures hurried away, toward the street. He knew he didn't have a shot. Teeth gritted in frustration and pain, Eldon held his shirt tightly to the wound in his stomach. It hurt, but not as much as he would have expected. Perhaps he wasn't injured that badly?

He waited until he heard the rumble of the Mercer's engine then crept back to the garage, crawling in through the opening Malcolm had made. He savagely kicked the body at the base of the stairs, cursing the interfering sailor for ruining his chance to kill his stepson. Upstairs, Eldon ripped the sheets off the bed and tore them into bandages which he gingerly wrapped around his torso. Back downstairs, he opened the boot on the Pierce Arrow and removed a small valise, changing into a clean shirt. He'd packed a few articles of clothing in case he had to lie low until he forced Malcolm to pay a ransom for his lovely fiancée--not that he would have given her back. Eldon's face contorted with anger. The whelp and his red-headed bitch had ruined everything! First Elizabeth, now the two of them, had thwarted his plans.

The pain in his stomach was nothing compared to the burning rage flowing through him like lava. He climbed into the car and backed it right through the doors. The rusty hinges gave way with a wrenching screech. The rotted wood shattered and flew in all directions. Eldon knew the glossy shine of the car would be destroyed, but he was past caring.

He stopped long enough to splash petrol from his spare can around the garage and over the body. Standing at the door, he flicked a match and threw it, jerking back as the vapors exploded. Backing down the alley, he could already see flames licking hungrily up the walls.

A quarter of an hour later, he eased the Arrow off the main road and down an old wagon trail meandering through the forest at the back of the DuMont estate. The moon had dropped below the horizon leaving the night dark as ink. The track was familiar--he'd used it for frequent hunting excursions--so he didn't need headlamps. "Tonight I'll be doing a different kind of hunting," he muttered. Eldon recalled the last time he'd pursued Malcolm through the woods. It was sheer luck he'd spotted the horse and rider on the river trail. It was sheer bad luck he'd been unsuccessful in killing the hotheaded pup then.

Now he had the chance to rectify the situation.

The fenders of the car were mangled by the time Eldon coasted to a halt. Brightly lit windows glowed in the distance. There weren't any cars visible on the curved drive, and he assumed the party guests had left. The journey from town had given him time to think over his options. As usual, he'd managed to come up with a plan to get out of trouble. Of the people who could bring him to grief, three were dead--never to talk again. The other three were there, in the house. If he disposed of Elizabeth, Malcolm and, sadly, the lovely Bridget, and without Eleanor, Carlisle and the *Titanic* crewman, there would be no one to stand witness against him. He would have more money than anyone else in the state. He would be untouchable.

Chapter 44

Malcolm sat next to Bree, their thighs pressed tightly together, one arm pulling her close, his other hand entwined with hers. She still suffered bouts of tremors and he had no intention of letting her out of his sight any time soon. Elizabeth sat across from them in her favorite wing back chair. A thick-set, stately man stood in a protective stance behind his mother, a proprietary hand on the back of the chair, near her cheek.

"I can't believe Eldon would do all this." Elizabeth shook her head. "How could I not see the evil in his soul? I must be the thickest..."

"No, Mother. None of us realized how deranged and dangerous he's become. He's very good at masking what he really is," Malcolm said.

Chief Fletcher spoke up, "I've got every man on the force out searching for him. He can't get far if he's injured."

"Thank you, Ernie. I hope you warned them not to take Eldon for granted. If he can't talk his way out of this, he won't hesitate to kill, especially if he's cornered," Malcolm cautioned.

Chief Fletcher looked back at him grimly. "I gave them orders to shoot if needed. They're also not to go out alone. We're all a tad jumpy. Things like this don't happen much around here. Except for Madame Zubrinsky's place, there ain't much crime around here. Beggin' your pardon, Elizabeth." He blushed to the roots of his gray-brown hair.

"Oh, Ernie, don't be silly. As if I and most of the other women in town don't have our suspicions of Mrs. Zubrinsky."

"I've already told her she needs to close the place down by the end of the month. When she said she was helpin' poor girls who didn't have husbands, we all felt sorry for them. But it got pretty hard to explain all those men going in and out all hours of the day and night. I guess I need to face up to the fact times are changing. Even places like Linton are riddled with criminals." The chief shook his head.

"I don't think it's as bad as that, Ernie," Malcolm said. "You've done a fine job over the years, and we appreciate it, don't we, Mother?"

It was Elizabeth's turn to blush as she met the chief's gaze. He looked at her with such longing Malcolm had to stifle a laugh. He felt Bree squeeze his hand and knew she had the same thought.

Headlamps flashed across the window. Chief Fletcher rose. "I imagine that's one of my boys. I'll go see what they found out." He hustled out of the room.

* * * *

Bree sipped her cognac. The fiery liquor burned all the way down, leaving her with a comfortable warmth. She had been shivering violently by the time they arrived at the house, as much from delayed shock as the fact she had no coat in an open car barreling through frigid night air. When they arrived, Elizabeth observed their disheveled condition and marched them into the parlor where she poured them generous snifters of the liquor. While they settled, she shooed the few remaining guests from the house with a promise to have another party soon, assuring them *it* would be attended by the guests of honor. One of the guests, Ernie Fletcher, was the chief of police. He and Elizabeth listened in amazement as Malcolm related what he knew of the story. Bree awkwardly tried to explain how she came to be in the Rolls Royce without bringing up seeing Malcolm with Melody. She was still confused about that episode, but with his arm tightly around her, she no longer had any doubts about Malcolm's love or intentions.

"Carlisle must have been in on it with Eldon," the chief said. "I wouldn't have expected that of the boy."

Bree nodded. "Apparently Eldon told him to get me into the car in whatever manner necessary, and I played right into his hands. Once he realized Eldon was up to something, Carlisle tried to stop him." She shivered at the memory of the violent attack on the poor chauffer.

"Why *did* you leave the party, Bree?" Malcolm asked, leaning close and compelling an answer with his intense regard.

As the others observed her expectantly, she felt her cheeks flame.

Closing her eyes, she said as quickly as possible, "I saw you and Melody in the garden. Eldon told me you'd decided not to marry me. I wanted to get away." She pulled free of his grip and clasped her hands in her lap. She looked down, embarrassed that her foolishness had caused all this turmoil.

Malcolm reached over and reclaimed her hands. "Bree?" She refused to respond. He gently tipped her chin up. "Eldon tricked Melody as well. He told her I wanted to marry her, instead of you. I only went into the garden with her because she told me she needed to talk about her father's mill again. Nothing more."

Bree saw the glow of love and tenderness in his eyes. It seemed impossible he could be lying to her. In a small voice she said, "I saw you and Melody in the garden yesterday, and then again tonight. And Eldon said--"

"Whatever Eldon told you was a lie. There's nothing between Melody and I except a business arrangement with her family. I swear that's all we talked about yesterday, and while she may have had a different idea tonight, she doesn't anymore.

His voice was so firm, and his gaze so sincere, all doubts disappeared. She laid her cheek against his shoulder, her hand on his chest.

"Oh, how very touching." Eldon said as he stepped silently into the room.

Chapter 45

Elizabeth gasped and started to rise.

"Sit down!" Eldon snarled. She cringed and sank back.

Malcolm tried to put his body between the pistol in Eldon's hand and Bree.

"Always the hero, eh, Malcolm? Not this time. I've had enough of this family. Little Percy, the milksop, always crying to our parents when he caught me having a little fun. It was because of him they sent me away to school. But I got even with him, just like I'll get even with you. Percy of all people should have known better than to trust me. But he was stupid, stupid, stupid." Spittle flew from Eldon's mouth as he ranted. "The fool eagerly drank my token gift of wine, happy I'd decided to bury the hatchet, as it were."

The revelation of the true cause of his father's death hit Malcolm like a brick.

"I would have liked to bury the hatchet in his head!" Eldon spat then closed his eyes, clearly struggling for composure. His gaze flicked to his wife. "So I married his insipid widow, the beautiful

Elizabeth, the woman who refused to die." He sneered at her gasp of outrage. "If there had been any way short of marrying you to get my hands on Percy's fortune, I certainly would have taken it. Listening to your simpering conversation nearly made me want to take the poison myself. But that would have been a great loss, unlike you."

Malcolm seethed at the words. Bree tensed beside him and he grabbed her arm, fearing she might make a rash movement. Eldon expanded his smirk to encompass them all. "But enough idle chit-chat. You, my dear Elizabeth, can join your beloved Percy in death at last, and the two lovebirds here will have the opportunity to spend eternity together, if you believe all that church clap-trap."

He straightened his arm, the pistol centering on Malcolm. Eyes wild, Eldon tightened his finger on the trigger.

Bree tried to shove Malcolm out of the bullet's path as, for the second time that night, the report of a shot echoed in their ears. And for the second time, they watched Eldon slump to his knees and fall face first. Chief Fletcher stood behind him, service revolver in hand.

Elizabeth rose to her feet and rushed into the waiting arms of the officer. Malcolm turned to Bree and pulled her shivering body tightly against his chest. She leaned back and looked at him, searching his face intently

"I'm fine," he assured her. At her skeptical expression, he bent down, his lips meeting hers, giving her the best kind of reassurance.

* * * *

Ernie cleared his throat. Bree and Malcolm were roused from their bliss and reluctantly parted. Overwhelmed with a euphoria she'd never experienced, Bree wondered if she was intoxicated from the cognac, or Malcolm's love.

Chief Fletcher had a wide grin on his face as he watched the two lovers. "Pardon me, kids, but I do believe we'd best take care of a few things right now, before you all get too involved there."

Bree giggled and looked up at Malcolm. She could have sworn he blushed.

Malcolm gave her a wry grin and stepped away, keeping her hand snug in his own. "I suppose you're right, Ernie." He stared dispassionately at his stepfather's body as deep crimson blood spread across the marble floor.

Just then, Anderson and Bertie rushed in. Their eyes widened at the sight of Eldon sprawled in the claret pool. The ever-imperturbable butler recovered quickly. "Do you wish me to call the police, ma'am?" Anderson asked, then realized Ernie was standing next to his employer. His composure cracked. "Er, that is, I suppose--"

Malcolm took pity on the man. "Ernie will take care of the police, Anderson. I think what we need are blankets, a bucket of soapy water and a mop." He turned to the police officer. "Any reason we can't get this cleaned up and move Eldon to a more suitable location?"

"None at all. Better make it a canvas, though, not a blanket." The servants headed off to find the materials requested.

As Ernie stepped into the foyer and called the police station, the other three silently surveyed the body on the floor. Malcolm spoke first. "The man should have been on stage. I've never known anyone as capable of hiding their true nature as Eldon. I hated the man, but I never suspected he could have killed Father, or planned our deaths so callously."

Elizabeth shivered. "To think I lived with him these years. He's a monster!"

Ernie returned in time to hear the comment. He pulled the older woman under his sheltering arm. "I've known Eldon all my life. Didn't like him when we were growing up. He was mean. Sneaky like. Percy suffered from Eldon's pranks more than anyone, but he never made a fuss about it. Most summers we would find pets that had been tortured and killed, and I always wondered. Guess I should have paid more attention."

Malcolm shook his head. "You were a kid then too. And you can bet Eldon would have had a story to explain away any questions."

Bree snuggled close in his embrace as he continued, his voice tinged with sadness, "I wonder who besides Father got in his way? How many others has he hurt or killed?"

"You can bet I'll be lookin' into that. I don't suppose it matters much now, but if there's families out there wondering about someone who's missing, I'd like to give them an answer, one way or the other."

Elizabeth pleaded, "Find Eleanor. I never believed she would just leave us. She had no family in France or England and I'm sure she had no money." She gripped his arm tightly. "Try to find her, please."

"I will."

Malcolm frowned. "You know, while we were in Europe I read some novels by two Frenchman. I forget their names. Their stories had a villain named Fantômas. He did all kinds of horrible things, but never considered anything he did bad. They were just things he thought he needed to do to make his life better. He even killed his own son. He adapted to fit any situation and no one knew what he was really like. I think Eldon was the same--he had no conscience."

Ernie nodded. "I think you're right." He took a deep breath, as if to clear his lungs from the foulness Eldon had become.

Elizabeth spoke up. "I suggest another strong drink for all of us, but perhaps we should partake in the library?"

They trooped down the hall just as Anderson and Bertie returned. "I'll join you in a moment," Ernie said, and turned to help the servants.

Chapter 46

The police left in the wee hours of the morning, taking Eldon's body with them. Elizabeth retired to her room, but not before Malcolm glimpsed a gentle embrace between his mother and the police chief.

He stood with Bree in the doorway and watched the convoy of vehicles roll down the drive, then urged her down onto the lawn. They slowly made their way around to the garden where they wandered hand in hand, enjoying the mild weather and soothing quiet. The faint lavender tint of dawn backlit the big oaks lining the drive. Gravel crunched beneath their shoes.

"You know, this might be the first peaceful moment we've had since we met," Bree said.

Malcolm snorted with amusement as he pulled her into his arms in the shadow of a huge rhododendron bush. She melted against him. He felt the instant response in his heart, and his body. She turned her face up to him and he eagerly accepted the invitation. After several long, satisfying moments, he raised his head. "You know, my love, we've weathered more disasters in the weeks we've known each other than most people do in a lifetime. If the seas couldn't take us, and Eldon didn't manage to do us in, I think we've got smooth sailing ahead."

Bree touched the cross at her neck. "Amen to that."

Gaelic Vocabulary

Cobh: Cove

A shìorraidh!: For Heaven's sake!

a Thighearna!: Oh, Lord!

Dhuine!: Oh, Dear!

Gu sealladh orm!: My goodness!

a ghaoil: My love

Caidil gu math, caomh: Sleep well, beloved

Cailín: Colleen or girl

uafàsach!: horrible, terrible

About Terri Benson

Terri Benson is a history buff. And a romantic. And a chocoholic.

Each of these is a good thing, especially for a writer of historical romance. She loves to delve into the past and pull out little tidbits that make history real and allow her characters to come alive. All the foibles, attitudes and emotions of real people, because that's the way she see them. She will have attained her goal if readers close their eyes and see what's happening in her stories, if they fantasize about meeting someone just like the hero, and hope that something just as wonderful and exciting awaits them in their dreams.

Pick up Terri's books and go to places *almost* forgotten in time and meet some unforgettable people-- you'll be friends forever. Come on, ignore real life for a little while. You'll be glad you did.

Terri's Website:
http://www.terribensonwriter.com

CPSIA information can be obtained
at www.ICGtesting.com
Printed in the USA
LVHW011056170322
713617LV00010B/698